VICIOUS DOGS

HENRY BROCK

The first Lasker Investigation

ISBN: 978-0-9978256-3-3
© Henry Brock, 2016
Run Amok Press, 2017

RunAmok

What People Are Saying About *Vicious Dogs*

"Brock reshapes the traditional gumshoe persona in his debut noir novel. Brock's narrative is a pleasant mix of conventional and not-so-conventional hard-boiled noir, which includes a good deal of captivating dialogue and a pinch of banality amid a heavy surge of mystery-laced twists and turns that is all woven together with light humor. This balanced combination is certain to become a new favorite for noir aficionados."

-*Manhattan Book Review*-

". . . Vicious Dogs [is] an excellent, vibrant read, even though it does rather tarnish the image of Canada being an always-gentle country where the most untoward behavior is ordering an Americano at a Tim Hortons."

-*Mystery Scene Magazine*-

"Author Henry Brock's first novel Vicious Dogs takes you on a fast-paced journey, chasing a cat's tail through Toronto's avenues and alleyways in a tense noir mystery. . . This is one mystery that's sure to make you want to shower when you're finished."

-*The Walleye*-

"I bloody loved it. Henry Brock's Vicious Dogs is a brutal slice of lowlife noir that smartly blends Charles Bukowski with Eddie Bunker and breathes new life into the PI novel."
-Paul D. Brazill, author of *Old London Blues* and *Guns of Brixton*-

"A north-of-the-border PI story from down in the gutter. Derek Lasker is an investigator with nowhere to go but up, but watching him do so is great fun and will surely launch a long-running series. Spot on for PI fans who like a character to root for tangled in a messy investigation. Vicious Dogs hits all the right notes. This Dog bites!"
-Eric Beetner, author of *Rumrunners* and *The Devil Doesn't Want Me-*

"In *Vicious Dogs*, Henry Brock takes us on a tour of Toronto's seedy underbelly while reinventing the hard-boiled noir. The first (of, I hope, many) Derek Lasker Investigations delivers a whip-crack plot and devilish humor that goes down like a tall can of Molson's after a plate of poutine."
                    -Eryk Pruitt, author of *Dirtbags* and *Hashtag-*

For Tony, in place of the $20 I owe him

Chapter 1

I knew the place was a dump.

There were water stains on the ceiling and the smell of mold and mildew had me sneezing and was surely messing with my lungs. Probably did more damage than the cigarettes. The water in the shower smelled and was rarely clear. The carpet had bald patches. The bed had been slept on by generations of sleazeballs before I arrived six months earlier and I didn't like to think about what manner of bodily secretions would turn up if I examined the blankets under black light. I knew for a fact that at least one prostitute was working out of this motel. Not that I had partaken of her services. I couldn't afford the $40, even if her wasted appearance wasn't enough to turn me off. The television usually worked and that was the only decent part of the room.

As bad as the motel room was, it was better than the street. Unfortunately, as Hasid had made perfectly clear, if I didn't pay up for the past two-weeks' rent, I'd be kicked out. I couldn't be angry with Hasid; he wasn't in the charity business. He had two teenage girls a few years from college and needed every cent he could get. I understood. We are all grubbing through the world looking for a few cents to rub together. Like him, I was an independent businessman, though his fleabag motel was doing a better business than mine was.

Most of my income for the past year had come from being a guinea pig for pharmaceutical companies. Some of the tests paid pretty well—$200 a day for some of the long term ones. I'd made a cool grand the month before, during a five-day-and-night stay at the North York research facility. After the bi-hourly bloodletting, my arms were chewed up like a junky's. There were three major firms in the Greater Toronto area but I had worn out my welcome at all of them since they knew I had been involved in so many tests. I hated to think of all the crap that was floating around inside of me. Not so different from other times in my past, but being infested with untested drugs was a bit more frightening than the recreational variety that I had favored in my younger days. The closest thing to a high I got these days was when Hasid sprayed my room with some bug-killer from the Indian subcontinent.

Three days to come up with some money or I'd be sleep -ing in my car. With gas prices being what they were, the half-tank would have to last me. Maybe Hasid would let me leave it in his parking lot, and I could live out of the back seat and still use the first floor kitchen.

Christ . . . how had it gotten this bad?

I will admit that my thoughts were sometimes very dark. I often found myself looking into the suicidal abyss without fear and that frightened me. I used to love life but since my 35th birthday it seemed like everything I did turned bad. All my hours were spent trying to find enough money to get through the day. I was tired of it. I was just plain tired. I was growing tired of life itself, and that should have scared the hell out of me. But it didn't.

My cell phone rang. It was on the bedside table. I was lying on the bed staring at the splotchy ceiling while Sportscenter played in the background. The ringing surprised me since I was months behind on my bills and I assumed that the phone had been disconnected. Besides, I didn't know who would be calling me. I had become estranged from everyone who ever cared about me.

"Hello?"

"Is this Lasker Investigations?"

That threw me. I still had my license but hadn't gotten work as a P.I. since last year. I straightened up in bed.

"Yeah it is. How'd you get this number?"

"I saw your ad outside of Wong's Chinese restaurant."

"What ad?"

"It said that you did domestic surveillance."

Oh . . . that sign. It read:

LASKER INVESTIGATIONS
DOMESTIC SURVEILLANCE
SPOUSAL & TEENAGER ACTIVITY/INVESTIGATIONS
THE SURVEILLANCE SPECIALISTS

That last bit made Lasker Investigation sound like a big operation instead of just my 1992 Toyota Corolla and me. I used to do alright back when a couple of the big insurance companies hired me but that was years ago and they didn't have much need for private investigators these days, or at least that's what they told me when they let me go. I had bought the sign earlier in the year and had paid the owner of Wong's to let me hammer the wooden placard in front of his Kingston Road restaurant. Even though thousands of cars passed by it every day it had never gotten me any work. I had forgotten all about it. I had assumed that Wong had gotten tired of looking at it and had pitched it or some kids had taken it. I was so far in the dumps that I hadn't cared.

"Listen, are you available to watch my kid?"

"Of course," I said, my heart pounding with the anticipation of work. "We need to meet. Do you know the Tim Horton's near the Morningside Mall?"

"Sure. I need you on the case soon. I need your help."

The Timmy's was only a block away. "I can be there in ten minutes."

"Give me half an hour," he said.

Chapter 2

I was lucky enough to have done a load of laundry the previous day, so I was able to put on a clean pair of slacks and a dress shirt. Looked very professional, or so I hoped. I was watching my money so I had washed some clothes in the bathtub and hung them to dry. Hasid's wife Majzara did laundry in the basement of the office but even at $2 a load it was too expensive for me. I looked at myself in the rusty mirror that hung in my room: put up for those who used the motel as a sex stop I assumed.

I looked like hell.

I was never a particularly handsome man but when did I start looking so lousy? I was getting fat and I had bags under my dark eyes that I once thought twinkled with skeptical intelligence. My thick brow was becoming more pronounced and I looked positively Cro-Magnon. My hair used to be as thick and dark as an Adonis, but now it was as thin as Hasid's carpets and had streaks of gray at the temples. It was a little too long. I needed to scrape together $16 and go to a Superclips. It was also a little greasy. I was only washing it once a week to save on shampoo. Well . . . I say that but honestly: who was I going to see that I needed clean hair?

I had a half hour before I was to meet my perspective client and could have jumped in the shower but to hell with it. I wanted to work for him not date him.

To save precious gas I walked to the meeting.

As I walked into the quarter-full coffee shop fifteen minutes early I realized that I hadn't asked my caller what he looked like or even what his name was. I was definitely out of practice. Was I up for a case? I had no choice. I needed the money. If I didn't get something soon I would be working as a security guard for minimum wage and the depression that would bring might be enough to push me over the edge.

I thought I would drown my sorrows so I ordered a jumbo coffee with triple cream and sugar along with an apple fritter.

"That one at the front," I pointed out to the teenager taking my order, "With all the frosting." It had twice as much sugary coating as the other fritters so perhaps that would improve my mood. I took the tray to a table that gave me a good view of both doors. Would I be able to recognize a man who wanted to hire me to 'watch his kid' after seeing my sign in front of a roach-infested Chinese Restaurant? I knew my skills weren't what they once were but surely a man like that wouldn't be too hard to spot.

I had polished off my apple fritter (delicious) and was nearly done my coffee when a bald man in khakis and a baby blue golf shirt entered the Timmy's and began scanning the faces at the tables without a glance at the cashiers. Not here for the coffee or donuts, I thought. My detecting skills told me this was my man. The worry lines across his forehead were another indicator. He had the troubled look of a man desperate enough to hire someone like me. I stood and waved to the man and he nodded and walked to my table.

"Are you with Lasker Investigations?" he asked.

He didn't need to know that I was Lasker Investigations. "Derek Lasker." I held out my hand.

"Bob Linehan."

He sat down and sighed. He had his elbows on the table and his gaze was centered on my coffee cup. The pain in his eyes had me thinking that Bob understood the dark thoughts that had invaded my thoughts over the past several months.

"Do you want a coffee?" I asked.

He shook his head. His skin was flushed and I wondered if Bob was a drinker or in poor health. We sat there awkwardly for a minute.

"What can we do for you, Bob?"

"It's my son, Bob Junior. He's been hanging out with a new group of friends and . . . I've seen changes in him."

"How old is he?"

"Seventeen."

"What sort of changes?"

"Well . . ." He straightened up and sighed. He met my eyes briefly then looked away. "You have some sugar here." He brought his finger to the right side of his mouth.

I wiped the frosting away.

"Apple fritter," I said. I don't think Bob heard me. His eyes were wet and runny like uncooked eggs.

"He's become much more aggressive and withdrawn. We used to be close but now . . ." He shrugged.

"Not so unusual for a kid his age." I kicked myself for saying that. I didn't want to discourage Bob from hiring me for whatever he wanted me to do. "And you think this behavior is linked to his friends?"

"They're a rough bunch. My wife doesn't even like them coming over to the house. She says she's afraid for her safety." He looked around to be sure no one was listening then leaned close. "I'm not prejudiced but a couple of his new friends are black. The way they dress and act I think they could be gang members." He straightens up. "With kids these days it's hard to tell. They look and act like criminals even if they're on the honor roll."

"Is Bob Junior on the honor roll?"

"No. He's never been much of a student but neither was I and I turned out alright. Got my forklift ticket when I was his age and been working ever since."

With his soft appearance I would have placed him as some sort of desk jockey. My skills were poorer than I suspected.

"There's something else, isn't there? This isn't just about running with a rough crowd."

"No, you're right." He took a shuddering breath. "Two days ago I went into the backyard to mow the lawn and I found the neighbor's cat. It was dead and its head had been cut off, and I think Bob Junior did it."

Chapter 3

"I see," I said in my best passionless professional voice. Bob Junior had killed and beheaded the neighbor's pet. Kook City. That explained the look of pain on Bob Senior's face. "And you're certain that he did it?"

"When I found Mittens—that was her name. A nice tabby cat. I always liked animals and that cat in particular. I used to feed it anytime the Peterson's went away. Wouldn't let them pay me or anything. My wife is allergic so I liked being able to go over and sit and pet a cat. Very relaxing after a hard day's work."

"So after you found Mittens . . ." I prompted.

"I went inside and Bob Junior was playing a video game with one of his friends—one of the ones that scares my wife the most—and I asked to talk to him. He said that he was in the middle of a level." The anger on Bob Senior's face was plain to see. "We used to be good friends, all those early mornings of hockey practice, and now?" He shakes his head. "I said I needed to talk to him about something I found in the backyard and . . ." I thought Bob Senior was about to break down in tears. ". . . and when I said that someone had killed Mittens both of them started laughing like I had made a big joke! Then—then he said . . . the little punk bastard . . . he said 'someone guillotined that pussy!' and he and his gangbanger friend continued laughing and playing their game like nothing had happened."

"So what makes you think he killed the cat?"

"He knew that its head was chopped off, didn't he?"

"He could have found it earlier and not said anything."

"I don't think so. He always hated Mittens. I couldn't stay in the room with those two . . . two bastards, so I went out back and buried poor Mittens. I could have throttled Bob

Junior right then and there." The cold anger on his face had me believing him. "Derek, I'm—can I call you Derek?"

I shrugged. "Sure."

"I'm worried about him, Derek. I need someone to keep an eye on him. Your sign said you'd watch him, right?"

"Surveillance is our specialty," I said, quoting the sign.

"I'm worried that he's going to do something really crazy. He likes knives."

"Likes them how?"

"He collects them. Has a whole closet full."

That struck me. "A closet full of knives?"

"I didn't think it was strange. I mean, I used to carry a pocketknife when I was his age. Still do." He reached into his pocket and pulled out a very fancy folding knife. "Though this is a hell of a lot nicer than what I used to have." He handed it to me. "It's a Ron Yellowhorse. Very expensive. My wife gave it to me for out last anniversary."

It had two blades and a dark wooden handle with intricate silver inlay. "A work of art," I said as I handed it back. I didn't mention that I thought it a little strange that a wife would buy her husband a knife for an anniversary, but my wife left me after less than a year so what the hell did I know. "So what exactly do you want me to do?"

"Follow Bob Junior. I need to know what he is up to. Look, I've seen enough movies to know that when a kid kills animals that it could . . . evolve into something worse, right? I want you to make sure that he is not getting into anything that is going to destroy his life. I need you to help me get him under control."

I scratched my head. I saw some dandruff float down and I thought I really should have splurged with the shampoo and showered. "I can follow him and let you know what he is doing and who he is doing it with but I'm not a counselor. I can't do anything to keep him under control."

"I—I'm not a wealthy man but I can pay you to watch him and . . . and if he looks like he is going to do something like . . . like what he did to Mittens I want you to stop him, okay?"

I didn't like the feel of this case one bit and suspected that no matter what I did Bob Senior was not going to be pleased with the results. Just the same, I was in no position to be choosy.

"The sort of surveillance you are talking about sounds like twenty-four hours a day. Who knows what kids today get up to once the sun goes down?"

"Is that going to be pricey?"

I put on my most concerned look. "I can feel your concern, Bob, so we'll give you a great rate, okay?"

Bob Senior smiled and I could see the relief on his face.

"Thanks, Derek. I can see I did the right thing in calling you."

Then we made deal that I never would have taken back when the insurance companies were hiring me.

A lousy $175 a day. Pathetic. Less than half what I used to charge.

I shook Bob's hand after he gave me a $100 deposit.

Oh well.

It would keep me from living in my car and would allow me to buy some cigarettes on the walk back to the motel. A quick shower and then I would begin following Mitten's murderer.

Chapter 4

It felt good to be back in the saddle.

To be literal: it felt good to be back in the front seat of my Corolla listening to talk radio and smoking cigarettes while watching someone without them knowing they were being watched. It is an enjoyable thing to do if you can stand the monotony. I have a very high boredom tolerance, which is one of the things that makes me a good private investigator. Or at least that's what made me a good private investigator in years past. I'd been out of the game for so long that I was wracked with self-doubt. The best thing to do after getting bucked off a horse is get back on, right? There I was working as a P.I. again for a few short hours and already cowboy lingo seemed apropos. I didn't have a six-gun to protect me if the knife-wielding Bob Junior caught on that he was being watched, but I had ways of defending myself against cat-killing punks. I may not have been the physical specimen I was in my teens (where I was an all-city wrestler at 84 kilograms and an excellent defensive end in football), but I could still take care of myself if there was a showdown. Hopefully there would be no duels at high noon at any point in my future.

Bob Junior may not have been an 'A' student but he was attending school during my first day on the case. Bob Senior sent a photo of his son to my cell along with information about his car. It was a bright orange Honda Civic fully customized for street racing. The muffler alone probably cost more than I had earned in the past three months.

Bob Junior walked out of Winston Churchill Collegiate at 3:45 p.m. flanked by two friends. He was tall, several inches more than his father, and had an athletic build. He suffered from severe acne that was plainly visible from my vantage across the street. I zoomed in with my digital camera and took a picture of the group, all of whom wore the baggy clothes that had Bob Senior and his wife fearing that they were members of a gang. I had debated pawning the camera and the rest of my P.I. gear and had even gone so far as to bring the lot to the pawnshops on Church Street. The only thing that had kept me from doing so was the absurdly low rate they offered.

Bob Junior and his two friends got into his Civic and cranked up some bass-intensive hip hop (being out of touch with modern music, I didn't recognize the artist) . He squealed out of the parking lot, and I tailed them to a McDonalds. Being the consummate professional (and being hungry) I followed them in.

Anyone who longs wistfully for those high school days and would like to return to them must have forgotten just how boring high school kids are. I made sure there was a barrier between us to keep me out of their line of sight but sat close enough to hear each word of their inane conversation.

Was I ever that dull and dim-witted? Probably.

After forty-five minutes I was hoping that one of them would attack some unsuspecting house pet just to liven things up. Instead, all I got was vapid talk of videos games, girls, basketball, television, movies, hip hop, and cars. To keep myself interested during cases I keep very detailed logs. This is also useful since one never knows what information will prove useful later on down the trail. As I sipped my coffee, which tasted better than I expected from McDonalds, I made notes about the topics discussed. Though the talk was innocent and non-violent, the tediousness was excruciating even for someone like me, who spent many days lying on my back chain-smoking cigarettes while staring at the Rorschach test water stains on the ceiling. I used to marvel at all the things I could see there. Enduring their juvenile banality convinced me that I had earned Bob Senior's $175 by the time the three left the McDonalds ninety minutes later. Once I heard them beginning to make a move toward the door, I left before them so I would be waiting in my car ready to follow them out of the lot.

After dropping his friends at a tall apartment block, Bob Junior went to a white house close to the Scarborough bluffs. Home? I wondered. Again I was sloppy for not getting this sort of information when I was hired. This was a nice neighborhood and I thought they might even have views of Lake Ontario. I didn't know enough about real estate to know the value of the place but I bet $750,000 was a good guess.

At 5:30 a large SUV pulled into the driveway behind the Civic and Bob Senior got out. I slouched down in my seat as soon as he closed his door. He began scanning the street. Was he looking for me? Making sure I was earning my pitiful fee?

I didn't think I was spotted. He went inside and I wondered if the family was going to settle in for a nice dinner. Five minutes after the thought entered my head, both Bobs left the house screaming at each other, son followed by father.

I raised my parabolic microphone and listened in over the headphones They were part of the package I had purchased back when I worked for the insurance companies and could slip the bill in as part of my expenses. I had all manner of trinkets that I hadn't had the heart to part with for five cents on the dollar to those skinflint Russian pawnbrokers. Or were they Armenian?

First I heard Bob Junior who was turned toward me.

"Fuck you!" he said. "You are such a hypocrite!"

Bob Senior said something but I couldn't make it out since he was facing his son and must have been speaking in quieter tones. The two men were walking toward the cars in the driveway.

"You know you are!" said Junior. "You tell me to not speak to her that way when you treat her like dirt!"

Again I couldn't pick up Senior's reply.

"You know exactly what I am talking about! Think about it! Now move your truck so I can get the hell out of here."

"You're not going anywhere," Senior said, turning so my mic could pick him up.

"No? Do you want me to go back inside and tell mom about who I saw you coming out of that motel with last week?"

Even from across the street I could see Bob Senior flinch as if he had been slapped. He then stepped close to his son and said something that I wish I could have picked up. He got into his SUV and backed out of the driveway, allowing Junior's orange Civic to roar out. I started my Corolla and followed, struggling to keep up.

Judging by the heated exchange between the Bobs, not all the knives in the Linehan family were made of steel.

Chapter 5

Bob Junior didn't go far: just a few blocks where he parked in a strip mall (certainly no shortage of those in Scarborough). After slamming the door of his souped-up import, he stomped toward a door above which hung a sign stating in four white block letters on a green background: DOJO.

The martial arts gym was on the second floor so no chance of my microphone being able to pick up what Bob Junior was doing inside. I was itching to rig some of my surveillance toys in his Civic but didn't want to risk doing it in daylight. I made a note in my book that Bob Junior was inside the dojo from 5:41 p.m. until 6:18 p.m. and that he came out with a short and hugely muscled man. He was a pit bull without a neck. Muscles connected the tips of his shoulders with his skull. He had a crew cut and was a generally freaky-looking individual. It would take more than one of Bob Junior's knives to stop this monster. Stab him and the mini-giant would smile.

I brought up my parabolic mic in time to catch Bob Junior ranting.

". . . gets to me. Don't know what to do sometimes. I know you say focus is the key to—"

"Focus is the key," said pit bull is a raspy voice, "to everything." He was staring intently at Junior. "Without focus we're particles drifting aimlessly, powerlessly through the cosmos. With focus we become lasers. Become unbreakable steel. With focus nothing can stop the human will."

Bob Junior nodded. I couldn't be sure but he looked almost bashful. "Thanks, Ray. I gotta bolt."

"Be strong."

"Always."

Bob got into his Civic and roared away. As I started my car to follow him Ray the pit bull looked at me with suspicion. He met my eyes and I could feel his beady orbs (like laser beams?) bore into my optical cavities. I looked away and pulled out quickly, hoping he didn't get a good look at my face or my license plate number. He scared me; I am not ashamed to admit it. It seemed that Bob Senior was correct: his son did have some dangerous friends.

It was the next morning during the 680 News seven a.m. broadcast that I learned I might have screwed up very badly. After Junior left the dojo he had driven around for three hours. There was no way for me to know if he was driving at random or for some purpose that was unclear to me. All I knew was that my gas tank was getting lower and lower as Junior rolled through Scarborough, often traveling the same length of road over and over. I was hoping that he would need to stop as well, but apparently those Civic tanks hold a lot of fuel. It wasn't like the old days when I had people I could call to back me up. Besides, I couldn't afford to hire help. As my fuel light clicked on I had no choice but to pull into a Shell station. I wanted to fill up quickly and try to catch up to the Civic, but as I put the gas nozzle in the tank and pushed the trigger nothing happened. A scratchy disembodied voice said, "You need to come pay first." I ran inside and tossed $10 at the clerk. I was rushing out the door when he called after me, "Want a receipt, mister?" which stopped me. If I was only making $175, Bob Senior should be picking up my expenses. All in all, it took me over five minutes to get out of there and by then Bob Junior was long gone. I cruised around for an hour, and then parked on Kingston Road where he had driven twice during his cruise but no luck. At 11:30 p.m. I went back to his house and parked where I had a clear view. Bob Senior's SUV was there (an Escalade I noticed—a pricey car for a forklift operator—and I won-dered what his wife did for a living) but not the Civic. My anxiety lessened when the orange car drove into the driveway and Bob Junior got out and went inside the house. After an hour, during which there was no movement inside the house, I surreptitiously made my way to his car to affix the devices that would ensure I would not lose my quarry again. It even allowed me to catch some sleep since I knew that the moment the Civic moved I would be alerted by the tracking device.

I woke just before 7:00. After peeing into a water bottle and putting it into the back seat (the glamour of the stake-out), I lit my first cigarette of the morning and clicked on talk radio. When the news began at the top of the hour my heart dropped.

"A grisly discovery this morning outside of Winston Churchill Collegiate on Lawrence Avenue East. A custodian arriving at the school just before 6:00 a.m. found the head of a house cat mounted on a stake outside of the school's front entrance. Police have cordoned off the area and are not commenting at this point."

My heart was somewhere near my belt line. Several questions immediately popped into my mind.

Did the head belong to Mittens?

Did Bob Junior put the head there?

What was I going to tell Bob Senior about the incident?

Was I going to be fired for losing track of his son?

Was I going to be kicked out of Hasid's motel?

Was I going to end up on the street?

How insane did one have to be in order to mount a cat's head on a stake outside of one's high school?

That last one was easy enough to answer.

Pretty damned insane.

Chapter 6

"What do you mean you needed to stop for gas?"

I had decided to gamble and use honesty on Bob Senior. It wasn't out of any high moral standing on my part, simply that all of the lies that I came up with made me sound even more incompetent than the truth.

I remained outside of the Linehan residence and was talking to Bob Senior on my cell. He told me his son was still sleeping and he had just heard about the cat on CBC Newsworld.

"We don't even know if the head belongs to Mittens," I suggested.

"What? Are you kidding me? What other cat do you think it would be? Do you think there are that many cat heads out there?"

"And we don't know whether Bob Junior did it."

"Who else would it be, Derek? It was in front of his school for crying out loud! We would know if he did it if you had only done your job!"

The media had swarmed the school and every station had cameras on the scene but the police had set up a tent to keep the image of the cat head off of the morning news. The story was just the sort of thing that made news people salivate since it brought the abject cruelty that lies in the heart of man to our Canadian metropolis. Who isn't fascinated by the human dark side? It was something out of "Apocalypse Now", said one commentator on 680 News, though I don't remember cat heads in the film. Humans, sure.

"Needing gas was an unfortunate turn of events," I told him. "I'm not able to have more than one agent on the case at any given time due to the low fee we agreed upon."

"You promised me twenty-four hour surveillance!" He yelled in that way that people do when they are trying to be quiet: a muffled angry tone. "If you couldn't deliver you shouldn't have—"

"Look, Bob, it was an unfortunate circumstance. There's nothing we can do about it now. I do have a few questions I want to ask you that will help us as we move forward." I closed my eyes. If Bob Senior was going to fire me, this is when it would happen; with a 'We are not moving forward you incompetent dandruff-ridden hack!' But thankfully he sighed and said:

"Okay. What do you want to know?"

"Does Bob Junior belong to a martial arts gym?"

"Yes, or at least he used to. I don't know if he is still going."

I gave the address and Bob confirmed that it was the place. I described the pit bull and asked if he was an instructor.

"I don't know. Not like Bob Junior wanted me around, just wanted me to pay the fees."

"Does he work?"

"I wish. Kids today . . . no sense of purpose. All they want to do is play video games."

"That car he drives can't be cheap. Did you—"

"That's none of your business! I hired you to keep an eye on him not to pry into our family life!"

With a click he was gone. I hadn't even had a chance to ask the most important question of all: When can I come to get more money? I decided I would give Bob Senior a few hours to calm down and then call him back.

The school was closed for the day, a fact I learned from the news. Was that why Bob Junior did it? If he did indeed do it that is. Did he have a big test that he wanted some extra time to study for? Seemed like a stretch.

I made notes in my book that Bob Senior left his house at 8:07 a.m. and then nothing for several hours. I ate some cold french fries that I had left over from McDonalds. Bob Senior didn't want me to pry into his family's life but I was a naturally curious guy. I wanted to get a look at Mrs. Bob Linehan, to see the mother of a future psychopath. Would she fit the stereotype? Be one of those teary mothers who had no idea her son was crazy, proclaiming that he was a good boy, that no one understood him but her?

The mayor of Toronto, never one to miss an opportunity to grab the spotlight, was quick to weigh in on the cat head. He called it one of the most heinous acts perpetrated during his tenure as mayor and that the full force of the law would come down upon the individual or individuals who carried it out. It was the sort of speech you would expect. He decried the fact that the head was placed in front of a school where children go and talked about the need to increase the number of police patrolling "our neighborhoods".

I was beginning to feel the need for a coffee and for some food other than twelve-hour-old french fries. And to make use of a washroom instead of a water bottle. The toys I had installed left me confident that I would be able to find Bob Junior if he left. Then again . . . if he left in another vehicle or on foot I would be in trouble. I couldn't afford to lose him again or Bob Senior would certainly fire me. I was regretting taking such a lousy case. I was completely unprepared. Why hadn't I packed a big thermos of coffee? Brought a bag of food? Just more evidence that I was woefully out of practice.

As I was debating whether to risk dashing out to a Tim Horton's, a nugget on 680 News sent my greedy mind whirling.

"Even though the case is only a few hours old," the announcer said, "the Humane Society has announced that it has teamed up with several donors and is offering a $10,000 reward for information that leads to the arrest and conviction of the person or persons responsible for the incident outside of Winston Churchill Collegiate."

Ten thousand dollars!

Imagine it!

I'd be able to get a real apartment instead of Hasid's fleabag motel! I could get my career back on track! Wash my clothes in an actual washing machine instead of a filthy bathtub! I'd be able to afford a $16 Superclips haircut!

I wondered if I knew enough to turn in Junior right then.

Chapter 7

I stopped at the same Tim Horton's where I had met with Bob Senior, and after washing up in the rest room I ordered another jumbo triple-triple and an apple fritter. I still needed a shower (even I could tell that I was beginning to smell) but first I wanted to go to Winston Churchill Collegiate to inspect the scene of the crime. As I left the coffee shop I quickly calculated that the reward money would buy me 5,263 jumbo coffees. That was a lot of coffee, and I wanted it. My eagerness to find every piece of this puzzle had me postponing my shower. I would have plenty of time to shower later.

I had heard on the radio that the police had cordoned off the area, so I had doubts as to whether I would be able to determine if the head belonged to Mitten's, but the $10,000 was more than enough to make me try. I spent the drive trying to come up with a good line of bullshit that would allow me to peek inside the police tent to see if the cat was a tabby. Since there were likely thousands of tabbies in the Greater Toronto Area there was no way I could know if the tabby was indeed Mitten's but the odds would be strongly in favor of it.

The school was on Lawrence Avenue East, which was only a few minutes' drive due to most of the early morning traffic going east to west into downtown Toronto, not north to south.

Television vehicles and police cars clogged the lane in front of the high school. The street entrance was not closed off but was so crowded that it was hard to get through. Large media vehicles with tall antennas sticking out of them were surrounded by camera people and reporters, and numerous cops and police vehicles filled the street. It took me ten minutes to get past the school and find a parking space three blocks away.

Taking my tracking device that would alert me if Bob Junior's car moved, I walked back to the school and upon stepping onto the grounds and up to the yellow tape I was immediately approached by a cop with an outstretched hand, palm facing toward me.

"School's closed sir," she said in that polite yet threatening manner that all officers are trained to employ.

"I know that. I'm . . . uh . . . investigating the cat."

Her face may have been pretty, but not in the polyester uniform with a bullet-proof vest or with the scowl she was giving me. "Investigating the cat?"

"Yeah . . . well I guess you could say I think I know who the cat might be and I came down here to find out if my suspicions are correct."

The officer, Papineau, said her name tag, looked me up and down and I bet she was wondering if I was the sort of crazy person who would put a cat head on a stake and then come chat with the cops about it the same way that arsonists often do. It also occurred to me that serial killers often got involved in the investigation that was searching for them, and I suspected that Papineau knew this as well. Did I look crazy? Well . . . I suppose I wasn't terribly fresh and clean at the moment, and the huge coffee and the prospect of $10,000 was making me a bit jittery.

"Look . . ." she said. "You need to move along. There is nothing for you here, except trouble. Are you looking for trouble?"

"Never." I smiled. "But still . . . it seems to find me."

Papineau didn't appreciate my attempt at humor, and I suspected I was moments away from a pepper-spraying or a billy club to the teeth when I saw a chrome-domed behemoth that I recognized.

"Hey!" I yelled. I stepped into the yellow tape and Officer Papineau held out one hand and placed the other on some item on her belt. Whether it was pepper spray, Taser, or some other torturous device I had no way of knowing.

"Stay where you are, sir!" she barked.

"I know him! Gord Grossman! Hey! Gord!"

Papineau glanced over her shoulder and saw that the huge bald cop was looking with curiosity in our direction. He wasn't in the blue polyester. He wore the much more bad-ass green of the Emergency Task Force: Toronto's version of a SWAT team. He wore weapons all over his body and generally looked like the sort of person who could have kicked the ass of ten or twelve hardened criminals without breaking a sweat. "Gord! It's me! Derek Lasker!"

His curiosity turned to a smile and he walked toward us. Seeing him smile did not in the least lighten his frightening visage. It was like looking into the grinning maw of a great white shark or the glaring white teeth of a snarling wolverine.

"Is that you, Lasky?" he said in a voice that reverberated like a tympani.

"None other, my man! Long time no see!"

"I thought you were dead," he said as he arrived at the yellow tape. Papineau, who was watching the exchange, appeared sad that she'd now been denied the opportunity to take me down. She looked back and forth between us as we talked as if wondering whether she would still be afforded the opportunity to beat me down. "Didn't you O.D. or something?"

"What? Who told you that?"

Gord shrugged his broad shoulders. "Don't remember. Was just something that was going around the old gang."

We had been close back in high school when we were both jocks. I was a defensive end and he was a tackle, and he used to burst through the line and crush many quarterbacks before they knew what hit them. One of the reasons my stats were as good as they were was that so many players on the offense ran frantically from him and into my waiting clutches on the right side of the defensive line. He was also an incredible wrestler, a national champion in the highly competitive super-heavyweight division.

Gord wasn't one of those gentle giants you hear about. He was a bad man who loved to throw his fists and dish out punishment to anyone who gave him half an excuse. The fact that the city made a psychopath like him a police officer told me its psychological tests needed revising. Who knows? Maybe the cops needed their own psychos to help combat the civilian ones. All I knew is he was often in the news after receiving commendation upon commendation, or for being acquitted of using excessive force, which happened on numerous occasions. I had lost track of how many people he'd shot so far in his career. Five or six. A shocking number in a country where most cops never draw their weapons over the course of their career.

He continued, "Word was that you hit the skids pretty bad once you stopped getting P.I. work and you weren't doing too good even when you were sucking on the insurance company's teat. By the looks of you, and the smell of you, I'd say you musta come pretty close to rock bottom, eh?"

The bastard just smiled at me and nudged Papineau who still looked at me like something wet and stinky that Mittens might have left it a litter box.

"Not really, Gord. Lasker Investigations is still going strong. Working hard on a case right now."

"Really? That's great!"

He was looking mildly impressed until Papineau piped up: "He said he's investigating the cat."

"What?" Gord's face was scrunched up as he looked down at me. "Investigating the cat? What the hell does that mean?

Who hired you? Mice?" He laughed at that *bon mot* and even the humorless Papineau joined in.

"Very funny. I believe that the killing of this cat is related to a case I'm working on."

"You know who did it?" he asked.

"I might."

He reached out and grabbed my once strong bicep with his huge right hand. "Then we need to have a long talk, Lasky."

He pulled me under the yellow tape and I found myself inside the hottest investigation currently on the Toronto Police docket.

Chapter 8

"Just like the good old days, eh Gord?" I asked as we walked down the high school corridor. To the right there was the trophy case and the two of us between wrestling and football (plus Gord was a champion shot-putter) had won our share of glory for our high school.

"You think high school was the good old days?" he asked. "I couldn't wait to get the hell out of there. My life didn't begin until graduation. Once I went to college that's when the real fun began." He smiled at me. "If you knew how much pussy I got in college you'd rip off your sack in shame, my friend."

"I doubt that."

"If only you knew . . ." He smiled and shook his head as he relived the memories. Outside of a classroom, Gordo stopped me with a huge hand on my chest and looked at me earnestly.

"I need to ask you something before I take you in there."

"Shoot."

"Are you high right now?"

"What? Of course not! I don't use drugs."

He fixed me with a look of disbelief. "You can't bullshit me, Lasky. I've seen it all. Crack heads. Dusters. Potheads. Coke heads. Juicers. Junkies. Boozers. Acid freaks. Shroom fiends. Tweakers. And you got the look, Lasky. It's written all over you." He took my wrist in his hand and turned my arm over, pointing at the needle marks in the crook of my elbow. "Don't know what you're shooting but it's nothing good."

I tried to pull my arm away but it was like anyone other than Arthur trying to yank Excalibur from that rock. "These are from some work I did at a pharmaceutical company.

They draw blood like . . . every two hours! I'm not on smack or anything else!"

He nodded, clearly not believing me. "Right. Your P.I. company is doing well and you're working as a guinea pig?"

"Well . . . everyone needs a little extra money these days right? Hell . . . with the stock market tumbling like it did a few years back a lot of us took a hit and—"

"Look, Lasky, don't shit me. I don't care about what you do. I just need to know if you are straight right now and not just riding some delusional wave and wasting my time. This case is drawing a lot of attention. The powers that be want it wrapped up *tout suite*, understand?"

I don't know whether he honestly thought I was on drugs or was just playing with me. He always was a power-tripper so I had no doubt that this habit was only heightened by the authority given to him as a member of Toronto's finest. "I'm clean, Gord."

"Okay then. Let's go."

The classroom, which had numerous pictures of Shakespeare and quotations from his works stuck to the walls (one in particular caught my eye: "Cowards die many times before their deaths, / The valiant never taste of death but once") had been turned into the nerve-center for the investigation into the cat head. I had been hoping to get a peek inside the tent but Grossman had led me into the building too quickly for me to suggest it. I admit I was a little nervous. Who isn't when in the company of that many cops? Even the completely innocent had to feel jumpy in such a situation.

There were a half dozen men talking in one corner and they looked up as soon as we walked into the room. Some of them were in uniforms with epaulets and I didn't know what they meant in terms of rank, but I could tell they were upper brass. Over eighty murders in the city last year and

I doubt that many of them got the treatment that this cat head garnered.

"What have you got, Gordon?" one of the uniformed old men asked. He had thick white eyebrows that made him look like a mutant or alien. More like antennae than hair.

"Lieutenant Hendrickson, this is Derek Lasker. He says he knows who did this."

"Well . . ." I didn't want to be spilling all I knew to this room. Surely I'd be losing any chance of securing a reward if I did! I needed to be cautious and be sure to protect my best interests. "What I said is I think I know who may have done it, and I came down here to find out if I was right."

"Well spill it," Hendrickson said. "We don't have all day."

"I have a question of my own before I say anything. Was the cat head you found a tabby?"

"That's none of your business," Hendrickson snapped. "You said you had something to tell us not ask us goddamned questions."

Every eye in the room stared me down and I felt increasingly uncomfortable.

"I heard on the radio that there was a reward so before I say what I know, I want to make sure—"

"You care more about the money than the public good, do you, Lasker?" the old man asked. Christ! He was as much of a hard-ass as Gordon Grossman. No wonder the big man did so well as a member of the force. "Where did you find him, Gordon?"

"He just showed up. He's a private investigator, or at least he used to be." Gord smiled at the old man. "He told Papineau that he was investigating the cat."

Hendrickson's eyes narrowed as he looked at me. "What the hell does that mean?"

"That's what I said!" Gord chortled. "Then I asked him who hired him . . . mice?"

Everyone in the room laughed except for Hendrickson who looked at me in much the same way that Papineau had.

"I don't trust this guy," he said. "Smells dirty. Literally and figuratively."

"I was on a stakeout all night. I came right here and I didn't have time for a shower and—"

"You were up all night investigating the cat and you still won't tell us who did this to it?" the old man asked.

I sighed. "Look . . . I don't know why you guys are pushing me so hard. I came here to help and you are acting like I am a criminal. I even went to high school with this guy and we were friends at one time."

"Is that true?" Hendrickson asked.

"Yeah, but not like we kept in touch. Lot of what I heard about him over the years makes me think he may not be the most stable, trustworthy guy."

"I will tell you everything I know but I just want to make sure that I'm in line for that reward."

"Okay, fine," Hendrickson said. "I'll personally see that you get it. Now tell me what you know."

"Before I do, surely you can answer the one question I have about whether the cat is a tabby."

Gord looked at Hendrickson and the old man thought about it for a moment then nodded.

"Yeah, it is," Gord told me.

"Then that makes it more likely that it is tied to my case."

Before I had a chance to share my information, I began to emit all manner of electronic noise. Within a moment of each other my cell phone began to ring and my sensor beeped, telling me Bob Junior's Civic was on the move. I looked at my phone and saw that it was Bob Senior.

"I need to take this." I walked into the hall and heard the cops calling after me but I ignored them. "Hello, Bob."

"Derek, look, first of all I need to apologize for flying off the handle this morning. This has been a tough time for me and my wife."

"I understand that." I needed to get to my car and find out where Junior was off to.

Gord opened the door and said, "We need to talk, Lasky. You don't want to piss off the men in that room. They can make our lives miserable."

I held up my hand and nodded. I made a motion that I would be one minute. I didn't know what I was going to say to them but I needed to make it quick so I could find Junior before he committed his next psychotic act.

Bob Senior continued, "Her and I talked about it just now and we decided that it wasn't proper of me to hire you to watch Bob Junior. We decided that there is no way that our boy could have anything to do with this whole mess and that we need to stick together as a family right now."

"But I am close to—"

"I know you did some good work and I really appreciate it. If you come by the warehouse I can pay you in full for all the work you did, okay?"

There was no way I was going to convince him and I figured I couldn't blame the guy. It was one thing to suspect your kid is nuts but maybe hiring someone to prove it wasn't the wisest thing to do. Besides, the prospect of the $10,000 meant I didn't need Bob Senior's measly wage, and not having to remain on the tail of Bob Junior would give me freedom to better investigate the case.

"Okay, Bob, fair enough. I'll stop by soon. I'll call to get the address." I hung up and turned to Gord. "Okay, time for me to spill the beans."

Chapter 9

"Sorry about that," I said as I returned to the room. "It was a call from my client." I had shut off my tracker for now since I didn't want them to know that I'd put assorted gizmos in Bob Junior's car. I wasn't entirely sure what I'd placed there was legal. I had the full attention of the men in the English room as I began to speak.

"I was hired yesterday by a man named Bob Linehan to watch his seventeen year old son who he was afraid was beginning to run with a rough crowd. I followed the kid and didn't see anything out of the ordinary. Just another Scarborough kid dressing like a L.A. rapper with nothing better to do than cruise the streets in a souped-up Honda Civic with friends that look like gangbangers, or maybe they are, I don't know. While talking to Linehan he mentioned that his neighbor's cat, a tabby that he was fond of, had disappeared. He didn't exactly ask me to investigate what happened to the cat but when I heard the news on the radio, I thought I would take a spin up here to see if the cat here could, by any chance, be his neighbor's cat. That's it. That's what brought me here before you."

The seven men looked at me blankly as I nodded earnestly, hoping that they would buy my tale. It wasn't worthy of Shakespeare but like his plays, it was fiction wrapped in a kernel of truth. I didn't want to give them the info about the beheaded cat in the Linehan's backyard since that was my key to the $10,000.

"Your client knows someone with a missing cat and when you heard about this case you put one and one together, did you? Great detective work . . ." said Hendrickson, his voice dripping with sarcasm.

"I knew it was a long shot but this place isn't too far from where the missing cat was from so I thought: what the hell, may as well check it out. Maybe you could take a picture to the family to see if it is their cat, Mittens. I can give you the address."

"You come to us with this feeble story and then tell us how to do our job?" Hendrickson snapped at Gord, "Why the hell did you bring this guy in here?"

"Like I said, he just showed up." Now Gord was looking at me with anger as well.

I suddenly felt like yelling 'Screw you guys!' and running out the door. I might have done it if I wasn't positive that Gord would love nothing more than to drag me back by my hair. Sure I had just lied to the cops, or at least didn't tell them the whole truth, but that didn't mean I deserved to be treated like a criminal did it?

"I never said I had any great information, just that I had a hunch about who this cat may have belonged to."

"Mittens," spat Hendrickson, who was beginning to look more and more incensed. I was becoming more and more certain that making a trip to Winston Churchill Collegiate was not a wise idea.

"That's right."

His eyes became slits and his lips twisted into an expression I had never seen on a human face, only on the cartoon character the Grinch. "And what about the tongue, Mr. Lasker? What does your brilliant private investigator mind tell you about that?"

"The tongue? I don't follow . . ."

Hendrickson walked up to me and got so close that I could smell his foul old man breath: stale coffee and a hint of the grave. When he spoke again, his voice was loud enough to almost be classified as yelling.

"Whose fucking tongue was in the cat's mouth, Lasker? Answer me that!"

I didn't have a smart come back for that one.

Chapter 10

Gord hustled me out of the room after Hendrickson's passionate outburst.

A tongue in the cat's mouth?

A human's tongue?

What would Shakespeare have to say about something like that? Wasn't there a line in one of his plays that went: 'Done to death by slanderous tongue'? I loved English Literature in my student days, though they were long past and my memory was woefully out of practice.

I suppose that horrific image of a cat head on a stake with a human tongue in its mouth helped explain the anxiety level the police felt and why they were pushing so hard.

"You made me look like a fool in there," Gord said bitterly as he led me down the hall.

"You can let go of my arm now." His big paw was clamped around my elbow. He let go but stopped me before we left the building.

"Lasky, why do I get the feeling that you didn't tell us everything you know?"

How to answer that one? "Well . . . I really need that $10,000, Gord."

He shook his head with disgust. "That's why I hate these goddamned rewards. You get greedy bastards willing to impede a police investigation to get their hands on some money."

"First of all, I'm not greedy. I just need the money. Secondly, I am not impeding your investigation." Or was I?

Gord stared at me without saying a word. Maybe he was hoping I would crack under his hard gaze but I was made of sterner stuff than that. "You know I could lock you up for keeping things from us."

"Who says I am keeping anything from you?"

"Don't bullshit me. I've been doing this job long enough to tell."

"Listen, I've got a case to get back to. The sooner I get back to it, the sooner I could unearth something relevant to this cat case."

His eyes were still on me. Was he wondering if I was worth taking into custody?

"Okay, I'll let you walk for now." He handed me his business card. "Call me the second you hear anything."

I nodded and put the card in my pocket.

He continued, "Listen, you didn't hear a thing—not a thing—that Hendrickson said, okay? If I learn that you mentioned the tongue to anyone you will have to answer to me, understand?"

"Deal." Who would I tell? Although I suppose the media might pay a pretty penny for that sort of info, but would they pay $10,000? Best to hold out for that sweet cherry.

"Now get the hell out of here."

And I made like a rocket and took off before the big bald thug changed his mind.

I pulled up in front of Bob Senior's place of employment to collect my fee. Would he be keen on paying me once I turned his son and namesake over to the authorities? Doubtful. Which explains why I was so eager to get the money as soon as possible.

A sign read DMC in stylized letters outside of his building. I had no idea what sort of place this was. I had called ahead so Bob was waiting for me in the parking lot. He wore that same anxious expression as the day before. I got out of my Corolla and shook his hand.

"It's been quite a day," he began. "Never thought I would want to hire someone to watch my son yet I did it and now here I am letting you go the day after taking you on."

"Why exactly are you letting me go? You said that you and your wife had talked . . ." Gord wasn't the only one who could sense when he wasn't being told the whole story.

It was painful to see the level of discomfort on Bob's face. He was twisted like a Tim Horton's cruller. He pursed his lips a few times before speaking.

"Not sure I want to get into all of that, Derek," he said at last. "Just didn't feel right, I guess. I mean, a man should trust his own son, right?"

He met my eyes and I could see the sadness and doubt that swirled there. I sympathized with the man. He had a good job, a wife and a nice expensive SUV but I would not have changed places with him. Well . . . perhaps if his wife was a total looker. But then again, would a gorgeous wife be enough to counteract a potentially psychotic son?

"I'm sure you're right, Bob. Who knows? Maybe Bob Junior is not up to anything bad and Mittens' demise was someone else's doing." Not that I believed that for a second.

"That's right. Maybe someone is trying to set him up." Bob was really grasping at straws.

"Exactly." Do you have any idea about who would want to do something like that? Does Bob Junior have those kinds of enemies?"

"Who knows? He could have. Kids these days. . . ." His weak attempt at a smile was painful to behold.

"We can just settle up and that will be that." I told him the grand total was $360 and I was glad that he didn't complain. I was worried he was going to try and get out of paying me for two days since I hadn't even put in twenty-four hours. Or maybe he would complain that I was charging him for the $10 in gas. But I suspected that he just wanted to get rid of me at that point. To be fair, I wanted to be rid of him too and be free to follow this case with the lure of $10,000 as my only consideration. I still wanted to follow Bob Junior and gather enough inform-ation to secure a conviction before I turned him over to law enforcement. I wanted to collect my measly $360 and get back to work.

I was pleased to see that Bob Senior had a mitt full of cash and he paid me in fifties and twenties.

"Feel free to call us if you have any further need for our services," I said. Again I used the plural to make Lasker Investigations seem like a proper outfit.

He shook my hand. "Thanks, but I just don't see that happening."

I got into my car and clicked on my sensor. Bob Junior's Civic had stopped and it wasn't far off. I sniffed my armpit and the pungency caused tears to come to my eyes.

A quick shower and then I would continue the hunt.

Chapter 11

I was looking forward to getting under that spout and enjoying a vigorous lather but Hasid spotted me as soon as I pulled into the motel parking lot. He walked to the car, waving and smiling. I knew from experience that he feigned a look of happiness when he was impatient. I knew what he was going to say to me (he would, of course, ask about the money I owed) and I was pleased to have a surprise for him. For once, I would not have to say: 'I will pay you soon! I promise!'

"Ah, Mr. Lasker! How are you today? I have not seen your car since last night and I began to worry!"

We shook hands. I may have thought this place was a dump but Hasid and his family were a delight. Even though I was far behind in my rent, he and his family continued to treat me with respect and had agreed to give me time to find the money to pay.

"I have been working, Hasid!"

"Oh! That is very good! You found another pharmaceutical company that did not know that you have been working with the others?"

"No, I found real work. Investigator work."

"Ahh, how good for you, Derek, to have real job back again. You have been not so good for the past weeks, yes?"

"Yeah, you're probably right about that." He was definitely correct and the depths of my depression was not something I wanted to think about, especially as I was breaking the surface, thanks to this case. "I got paid today so how about we go settle my bill?"

"Excellent," Hasid said. "But you are not leaving us yet, I hope?"

I wished I was, though I didn't want to say it. Hasid took pride in this place and wanted to make a go of this motel that he'd purchased earlier in the year. If he'd had the cash to invest I didn't doubt that he would have done something about the bald carpets, mold and foul smells. Perhaps the hookers, johns, junkies, drunks, adulterers, and those like me—the broke and nearly broken—didn't care much about the conditions of the rooms, or couldn't afford to care. The moment I had my $10,000 I would be gone in a flash, I was certain of that.

"No, Hasid," I said with a smile, "I would miss you too much." I wasn't completely lying either. He and his terribly sweet wife Majzara probably helped keep me alive over the past few months. Their contact reminded me that the world was not completely void of pleasant human interaction, of kindness and love. Now I don't want you to think that Hasid, Majzara or his two daughters felt love for me. It was enough to witness the love the family felt for each other, and for the work they all put into keeping this motel from bankruptcy, all while keeping smiles on their faces.

I'll admit that it never felt so good to part with money. Walking out of the office. My debt to Hasid was not completely cleared (I needed to keep a little of the $360), but I was pleased to have lessened it. It would be pleasant to not feel like a squatter and to wonder about how often Hasid and Majzara had contemplated kicking me out. If there had been demand for the room I'm sure they would have done so weeks earlier. I hated feeling like a deadbeat.

As I walked across the parking lot toward the stairs that lead me to my room, 208, a top of the line black Jaguar with tinted windows rolled past me, moving as slowly as the jungle cat might when stalking something that it wanted to eat for dinner. It parked near the stairs. From the front exited two black men who looked to be in their twenties and wore baggy gangster-wear. One of them held a large take-out bag from McDonalds. They looked at me with blank cold stares that made me realize that the kids that Mrs. Bob Linehan was so afraid of were nothing compared to seeing the real thing. These men dripped of menace and danger. These were not kids playing dress-up. From the back seat stepped a young blonde woman whose age was hard to determine behind the thick make-up. She could have been twenty or even five years younger. Her skirt was so short that it barely covered her bottom and I could not help but see that she wore pink panties. A halter top—the sort I thought went out of fashion at the end of the disco era—hugged her small breasts. She had to hang onto the door to pull herself to her feet due to her absurdly high-heeled, shiny white, faux leather boots. Sipping from a McDonald's cup, and without a glance toward my dumb-founded face, she awkwardly followed the two men up the stairs to room number 202.

My stomach sunk and the faint glimmer of optimism that I felt about humanity crashed to the asphalt around my feet.

A shower never felt so good.

Even still, I didn't linger, exiting the shower after a quick shampoo and scrubbing. A shave would have helped my appearance but it would have to wait. I had wasted too much time already.

I was on the trail of $10,000 and knew that if Gord or another cop fingered Bob Junior as the cat-killing perp, my reward would disappear.

I put on the least dirty clothes I could find and left 208.

I stopped at the top of the stairs to tie the shoe of my old Nikes that needed replacing. I could see my whitish socks poking through a gap at the toe of the right shoe. As I was straightening up the door to 202 opened and one of the men walked out. He moved toward me in a slow rolling gait. When he got close I saw that he was much younger than my initial impression, late teens, but there was still something old about him, as if he had been prematurely aged by life.

"What are you looking at?" he snapped at me.

"A new neighbor, by the looks of it." I even smiled and I could see my pleasantness pissed him off, as I knew it would. "Did you just check in?"

"None of your damned business." He pushed past me and down to the Jaguar that must have cost a fortune. I wondered what a man that young had to do to afford a car that would have strained the bank account of a Bay Street trader. It would take dozens of Humane Society rewards for me to afford such a vehicle. Bob Junior's Civic had impressed me and this Jaguar was in another league entirely.

Once he'd pulled out of the parking lot, I walked along the second level to the far stairwell and listened outside of 202 but all I could hear was the television. What was happening in there? Was the woman (or was she a girl?) in trouble? Was there anything I could do to help her? Did she need rescuing?

I shook my head to clear it. As troubling as I found this situation, I needed to put these people out of my mind and instead concentrate on a tabby's head with a human tongue, or I would forever be wearing holey sneakers and falling asleep alone in a water-stained room suffused with blooms of mold and mildew.

Chapter 12

I followed the tracer to the martial arts dojo that I'd visited the previous day. There, in the parking lot, was the orange Civic. I pulled my Corolla a few spots away and sat a moment trying to decide on the best course of action.

Since I was battling the clock, I chose to take direct action instead of my customary method of observing from the shadows. The lure of money will make any desperate person ignore their best instincts.

I walked through the door, above which hung a DOJO sign. As I climbed the narrow stairs to the second floor, I could hear the sounds of a class in progress. An instructor barked something out and what sounded like a room full of students barked back. At the top of the stairs I saw that the class of twenty or so wore a mishmash of training clothes: some wore simple T-shirts and sweatpants, others donned the more official *gi* of various colors. The instructor was the short and beefy pit bull I'd seen and heard talking with Bob Junior. He was leading the class in punches, lefts then rights, and he called out in what was either an animalistic grunt or an Asian language I didn't recognize. I scanned the class and didn't see Bob Junior among them. But then I spotted him behind the glass of an office. I skirted the padded area where the class was training and walked toward the office. The instructor's eyes were on me, and I nodded once as if it was perfectly natural for me to be there.

Bob Junior looked depressed.

He was seated in a chair to the left of the door. Hunched over with his elbows on his knees, he stared at the floor and didn't look up as I entered. This looked like it was the pit bull's office. On the walls hung several photos of him at various martial arts contests. In others, he posed in military garb, though whether it was Canadian military garb I couldn't tell.

"How's it going?" I asked to get Bob's attention.

He looked up at me with a questioning look.

"This a good school?" I asked.

"Sure."

"What sort of things could I learn here?"

"Combat arts of all sorts."

"The instructor out there, is this his school?"

"It's called a dojo."

"Dojo. Right." I smiled.

"Yeah, it's his school—Ray's. He's the best. I don't think anyone in the world could beat him in a fight. I keep telling him that he should get into the UFC and make some serious money but . . ." He shrugged.

"Maybe he makes enough money with this place." The dojo didn't look that impressive. Surely one could make a living teaching martial arts, but not like the money people were making beating each other senseless in the ever-growing sport of mixed-martial arts.

"He does okay I guess."

"Have you been here a long time?"

"Yeah. I teach some classes."

"Really? That sounds cool." I glanced out the door and saw that pit bull was taking a greater interest in me and my conversation with Bob Junior. "What do you teach?"

"Advanced weapon techniques."

"So I could learn to use nunchuks here?"

He looked up at me with his lip twisted, like he thought I was the complete idiot I was pretending to be.

"Nunchuks? No one uses those. I teach edged weapons. Knives. No fool with nunchuks could take down a man skilled with a knife. Knives are an underestimated weapon. Guns you need to reload. A knife keeps going and going."

I suppressed the chill that statement caused.

"You know, that sounds more my thing than what he's teaching out there. All that punching and kicking . . . doesn't help you much in the real world does it? But learning to use a knife . . . that's something that could help a man out in a scrape."

"You have any experience fighting?"

"Not formally but in my line of work rough stuff is sometimes necessary." I mentally kicked myself for saying this. After all, I didn't want anyone here at Ray's dojo to know what I did for a living and my reckless comment brought on Bob's obvious follow-up question:

"What line of work is that?"

Luckily I was a good and well-practiced liar. "Corporate security. White collar stuff. I'm on three months leave after working the big G7 summit. Always good to upgrade the skills, right?"

"Yeah, I guess." He smiled for the first time. "Never know when you might need to stick ten inches of steel in some lefty's ribcage."

He actually laughed at that and I joined along. Hardy-har-har.

In fact I was so absorbed in drawing Bob Junior out of his quiet depression that I didn't notice Ray the pit bull had left the class. I jumped when his deep voice spoke from my left.

"What's so funny?"

"This guy's interested in my edged weapons class."

"That so? That's not for new students, mister. It's an advanced class. You need to be in training for two years minimum before I let you take a class like that."

"He says he works white collar security."

"That so?"

I didn't like the way that both men were looking at me. Why is it that lately everyone stared at me like they were trying to decide whether to arrest me or beat me half to death? It was enough to make a man start to feel down on himself.

"Yeah. I saw your sign and thought I might take some extra training."

"Who do you work for?" Ray asked.

"A private firm." Best to keep lies as vague as possible. The details are what can trip you up.

"Uh huh. You work for some big firm and you come here to get training? Surely they could pay to send you to some pussy class downtown."

"I want the real thing. I like a place like this more than some neat and tidy martial arts club. I might work for white collar but I don't fit in with those types."

"He was at the last G7," Bob Junior volunteered.

"That so?" The suspicion had not left Ray's face. "Where was that at?"

"In the UK." Was the last one there? I had heard something about it on the news.

Ray corrected me. "It was Germany."

Oops. "Not every meeting is mentioned in the news. These people have so many backroom deals brewing that it would make your head spin."

"Bankers run this world," Ray said and it almost looked like his guard lowered slightly and his rant helped confirm that: "Used to think it was worse in the States, what with the Federal Reserve, which is a goddamned private corporation selling each dollar to the American government for the face value plus interest which leeches the country dry so a few families can get fatter and fatter, but now that I settled here I see that things aren't much better."

"Canadians are so far up the American ass," I began, "that when we look up all we can see are the feet of the Mexicans."

That seemed to do it. They both began laughing so hard

that tears ran from their eyes.

"That's a good one!" Ray slapped me on the back. "The feet of Mexicans! You're alright, buddy. What's your name?"

"John Sherman," popped out of my mouth.

"Well, John, if Bob is up for it, I say you're welcome to take his class." He looked at Bob.

"Why not?" was his reply.

"He's got a class tonight at 9:00. Me and him were going to grab a beer once this class is done with. How about you come along and give us the skinny on those bankers, 'cause I got theories of my own about those satanic bastards."

"Beer sounds good," I said. "And evil is something I've been learning more and more about with each passing day."

Chapter 13

My name was now John Sherman, and I had to remember it.

"But people call me Sherman," I told them after the waitress set down the pitcher of Molson Canadian.

"Like the tank," said Ray.

"Like the General," I countered.

"Mr. Scorched Earth!" Ray said, though I had no idea what he meant, so I just smiled.

"You ever do any serious dirty work for the corporations?" Bob Junior asked me with a hopeful smile on his face, wanting dirt.

"I never had to whack anybody, if that's what you mean."

"Really? Never?"

I smiled. "That was someone else's gig."

"Really?" Bob leaned forward, excited, eyes bright. "How did they do it? Silenced pistols?"

I shrugged. "What do you guys think?"

"Depends who is being hit," Bob said. "And where the hit is happening."

"And whether you want someone to find the body," Ray added. "Do you want to make someone disappear or to leave a bloody body to send a message?"

I nodded as if impressed. "The rest is just details."

"I got a question for you," Bob said, ". . . are you guys hiring?"

He and Ray had a good laugh about that and we all drained our glasses quickly. We sat there drinking our beer and I spun invented tales about an imaginary life. I wondered what my purpose was for being in that bar. As I had that thought, I began to feel nervous and wondered if this so-called surveillance expert was out of his depth.

It was that damn $10,000.

It had me trying to draw some incriminating evidence from two men who could both be stone cold killers for all I knew. I should have been sitting nice and safe in the front seat of my Corolla and listening on headphones to what these potential psychos were talking about, not sitting there drinking with them, bullshitting them, convincing them that I was a good guy and that slipping a ten inch knife into my ribcage was not the thing to do. I suddenly had the urge to flee, which I did my best to suppress. I had pretended to be other people a few times in the past— it's a good way to milk someone for information, but to do it well you needed to prepare. I knew nothing about this John Sherman, like the tank, like the general, who protected white collar moneymen, yet aired dirty laundry over a pint of beer in a Scarborough bar. What kind of person had I created? Who was he? I had no idea and ad-libbing was not my forte.

What if I got confused and thought my name was Patton or Grant?

Ray leaned close. "You feeling okay? You've gone pale."

"Yeah . . . just feeling light-headed. Must be hungry. They got good french fries in this place?" I waved at our waitress and ordered some. It gave me a chance to gather my wits and convince myself that I would be okay. That I could continue to juggle all the lies.

Ray refilled my glass.

I took a deep drink. The beer tasted great. "What got you into your line of work?" I asked Ray in a clunky change of conversation. I did not want to be at the center of an interrogation.

"What the hell would you care about that?"

"I'm a curious guy."

"Is that why you were parked in front of my dojo yesterday?"

Both he and Bob Junior were staring at me with intensity and again I felt like I was under a spotlight. "I was going to come in but decided to wait."

"You weren't following me?" Bob asked.

"Why the hell would I be following you?" I hoped my growing anxiety wasn't visible. "Watch you screw your girlfriend in the backseat of your rice-burner?"

"So you're a pervert, is that it?"

"Don't flatter yourself, kid. Want to know how you use a real knife not your figurative one."

That baffled the poor kid. "Huh?"

Ray helped demystify him. "He says he's not interested in your dick just on learning your skills with a knife."

"Oh. That's good," Bob said.

My french fries arrived and I began to shovel them in. Was it the rush of fatty calories that calmed my nerves? Or was it that I used stuffing a half-dozen fries into my mouth to cover my setting up a phone call to myself?

It rang and I swallowed quickly. I stood and pulled the phone from my pocket and said to them in a voice that suggested I was suddenly on duty.

"That's my boss." I took a few steps before answering the fake call. "Hey. Right. Who? How long? Okay. Why? Okay. Twenty minutes."

I slipped the phone back in my pocket and threw $20 down on the table. "Sorry fellas but I gotta split."

"What, momma calling?" Ray asked.

"Gotta go kill someone for the man?" Bob asked.

"Another day another dollar." I left without another word and had to admit that I was thrilled that neither of them called me back to the table. I had visions of them calling my bluff, or skipping that step entirely and instead tossing a few throwing knives into my back.

When I got outside to my Corolla I sighed, releasing some of the tension that had been building up in me over the past hour. I quickly got in the car and hit the gas. I pulled onto the street, drove around the corner, then pulled into the back parking lot and stopped on the opposite side of the bar.

I put on my headphones.

The bug I had placed beneath the table was working perfectly.

I smiled.

I loved being a snoop.

Chapter 14

If I was hoping to overhear something definitive that would convince me Bob Junior was Mitten's killer I was to be disappointed. That is not to say the conversation I was eavesdropping on didn't have its share of tantalizing revelations.

When I first tuned in the two men were talking about the "skanks" in the bar and about how a man would have to be crazy to get anywhere near them without being coated head-to-toe in latex.

"But that blonde over there, the one in red with the big jugs," Ray said, "might be worth suiting up for."

Then they discussed the relative merits of the current crop of fighters in the middleweight division of the UFC (not being a fan, I didn't recognize a single name) and Bob told Ray that he could take any of them. Ray said that he didn't have the connections to break into that racket and that one needed to be affiliated with a major training facility to be given a shot, and that at 35, he was too old to work his way up the ranks. Ray then thanked Bob for believing in him.

"Your belief in me, plus the belief the other guys have in me, is the most powerful thing in my life."

"You deserve it, man. You helped all of us."

"And you helped me. You guys are the best thing I got going in my life. Shit . . . things have been tough since they kicked me out of the marines."

"I know, Ray."

I couldn't be sure without seeing the body language, but from those three words I got the impression that Bob had heard this line of conversation before.

Ray continued, "When you become a marine, you're taught that you're a marine for life and you buy into that idea, and why the hell not? What's better than being a marine? It's the best goddamn fighting force the world has ever seen! 'The few. The proud.' Not just empty words to a marine. I still get chills saying it. You go into training and they tell you that you are no longer a man, you're a marine, right? So what the hell happens when they kick you out? If you're no longer a marine and no longer a man then what are you? You get me? You see the dilemma?"

"Sure."

"It's a tough one. A dilemma and a half."

"You've become something new, Ray. You're a teacher. A leader."

"Yeah . . ."

"And you've given me a chance to hone my skills. Where would I be without you and your dojo? Still throwing knives around my basement like an idiot, not knowing my potential."

"And you got plenty of potential. You got the skills. All you need to develop is the mindset."

"I'm working on it."

"I know it. I've seen your good work."

What exactly did he mean by that? Was the decapitation of Mittens his 'good work'?

"And you've given me a place to teach! Look, I even got professional bodyguards like Sherman interested! Who knows, he could open doors for me!"

No . . . I don't think so, Bob Junior. I wanted to close a cell on you and collect a healthy bounty for doing so.

"Maybe. But there's something about that guy . . ."

Uh oh. The pit bull was suspicious of me.

"Really?" asked the gullible young man. "But then again . . . I never would have guessed he was a bodyguard since he's pudgy. But I guess you can't tell by that."

Pudgy? I suppose I was . . .

"The second I saw him my bullshit detector started ringing off the hook. Don't know why. Something about the way he showed up at the dojo after I saw him in the parking lot yesterday. Doesn't feel right."

"You're paranoid."

"No, nitwit!" Ray snapped. "I'm concerned. I'm cautious, which is something you and your boys should learn to be unless you want to end up in the penitentiary!"

"Yeah, yeah, you're right. Sorry, Ray, I shouldn't act so casual."

"No you shouldn't—" he softened his tone "but you're still learning. You didn't have the benefit of marine training, right? Don't beat yourself up." I could almost see his pit bull smile as he said, "Not when you can beat others up instead."

"Cheers to that."

"And tonight we can get another look at this Sherman joker and find out if he is the real deal or—"

There was a pause and Bob Junior finished Ray's sentence.

"Or someone we can have some fun with."

They both laughed and I gulped. They wanted to have fun with me? What on earth did that entail? Whatever it was I knew that I wanted no part of it.

"Finish up your beer." Ray said, "And let's get out of here."

A couple of minutes later I saw Bob's Civic pull away with Ray in the passenger seat. I waited another ten minutes to make sure they weren't coming back to pick up something they forgot then I went inside the bar and pulled my bug from beneath their table.

On my way out I saw a busty blonde in a red T-shirt sitting at the bar. She looked quite drunk and very attractive. She was the only blonde in the place so this must have been the woman Ray was talking about. He would have coated himself in latex before touching her? He was foolish. I would have loved to touch her regardless of the conditions. If I wasn't almost completely broke, I only had $50 to my name, I might have sat next to her and bought her a drink. Right. How long had it been since I'd hit on a woman? Forever. She must have sensed me looking at her because she turned her head and met my eyes.

She smiled.

I smiled back briefly then walked toward the exit feeling very low and cowardly.

I had my hand on the door and was about to leave.

I was planning on going back to my room, perhaps stopping at the liquor store on the way for a big bottle of malt liquor, and deciding whether I had the courage to return to Ray's dojo for that night's knife lesson.

But something stopped me.

I didn't push open the door.

Instead, I surprised myself by turning and walking confidently to the bar and sitting next to the beautiful woman. She smiled as I walked from the door to the stool next to her.

"Welcome back," she said.

I looked at her and close up I noted that she was a bit older than I'd thought from across the room. Mid-thirties. She had full lips, high cheekbones, and a spark of intelligence in her eyes that was visible even behind the alcohol gaze. Her face bore some pockmarks that suggested this curvaceous woman was once a pimpled teenage girl. The thought didn't make her any less attractive. Quite the opposite. She was even more beautiful than I'd thought.

"My name is Derek Lasker," I said with a formality I hoped would make me seem a gentleman. "Can I buy you a drink?"

"I'm Irene Johansen," she said with a smile that made my stomach twitter, "And yes you can."

Chapter 15

Drinking beer in the company of a beautiful woman must be one of the finest things in the world. What did it matter that I couldn't afford to be buying both of us drinks? The pleasure that Irene's company gave me was worth spending my last dollar.

"I've never seen you in here before, Mr. Derek Lasker," she said once the bartender had placed our drinks in front of us. She was drinking vodka and cranberry and I was continuing with draft beer, but with a pint of Stock Ale from Mill Street microbrewery. It was more expensive than the Molson's and was far superior. I wanted her to know I was a man with taste and class, despite my slovenly appearance.

"That's because I've never been here, Ms. Irene Johansen." There was a painful pause and to fill it I said, "Johansen . . . is that Swedish?"

She laughed. "That's not a terribly original line."

I'm sure I blushed.

"I never meant it to be a line." But of course it was. Small talk was not my forte. "I'm genuinely interested."

"Are you really?" Her smiled turned coy and I suddenly felt nervous.

"Well . . . uh . . ."

Her laughter increased and she punched me on the shoulder. "Relax! I'm just fooling with you. My grandparents came from Sweden but my family is very Canadian. The only time my father feels Swedish patriotism is during the World Hockey Championships."

"But loving hockey is so Canadian."

"Swedish too I guess."

"As for me, I never cared much for the game."

"What? I don't believe it! A Toronto man who doesn't

love hockey? Incredible. Are you gay or something?"

"Nope."

"Wow. Shocking. A straight Torontonian who doesn't worship the Maple Leafs." She held up her glass. "Well cheers to you for having the guts to not like hockey."

We clinked our glasses.

"Before you start thinking that I don't like sports at all, a characteristic that I imagine most women crave in a man, I have to admit I like soccer. The World Cup, European Cup, I could happily watch every match."

And I used to do so back when I had money in my pocket and a group of friends. Nothing better than drinking pint after pint in a pub full of other fans and feeling that one was part of an international event. People from all walks of life, from every nation, would all be glued to televisions taking in the excitement. It was like those pictures of planet Earth from space: they reminded you that we're all stuck here on the same planet and not so different after all.

"Ah hah!" she exclaimed. "I knew there was a catch. What do you do for a living, Derek?"

"I run my own private investigator business."

"Ohhh . . . you own a business! And you're a private investigator! How exciting!"

"It can be." How could I not be pleased by her response? "But most of the time it's very tedious."

"Following up leads and questioning witnesses and that sort of thing?"

"Something like that."

"Strong-arming people who won't cooperate with your investigation?"

"Definitely." I laughed and she joined me. She had a lovely laugh. "It's one of the perks of the job."

"Are you on a case right now?"

"Yes. A big one, or a potentially big one. Have you heard

about that cat they found at Winston Churchill Collegiate?"

"I think I heard something about that on the news . . ."

"I'm working on something linked with that. It could be a big deal, a lucrative case for me. What do you do, Irene?"

"I work at Hopkins Design Centre, where I help people pick out new kitchens and bathrooms and that sort of thing."

"Sounds interesting."

"Please . . . it's dreadfully boring and you know it."

"But it sounds like it could be creative. I wouldn't know how to redo a kitchen or bathroom or any other room for that matter."

"Believe me, a semi-intelligent ape could do it."

Before she could continue my phone rang. I looked down and saw that it was Gord Grossman. Speaking of semi-intelligent apes, I thought.

"Sorry, I need to take this."

She smiled and raised an eyebrow. "A break in the case?"

"Could be." I stepped away.

I was shocked by the fact that she seemed to like me.

Was such a thing possible?

Was I actually interesting to such an attractive woman? The thought filled me with an emotion that had been a stranger to me for many years: pride.

I answered my phone.

"Lasky, It's Grossman."

"How are you, Gordo?"

"Where are you right now?"

I told him the name of the bar. I spoke in a quiet tone: "And I am talking to a gorgeous woman. She's had a bit to drink but she seems really into me." After the beers I had shared with Ray and Bob Junior and the pint I'd nearly finished with Irene, I was feeling a pleasant buzz of my own.

"Goody for you."

"Yeah, it's been a long time for me . . . I remember you used to have no trouble meeting the ladies back at high school. Is that still true?"

"Yeah. Women love cops, especially ones that are six foot five and make the news. Listen, Lasky, before things get out of hand are you ready to tell me everything you know about this case?"

Get out of hand? What did he mean by that?

"I don't have anything concrete, not yet, but I am working on it and getting closer and closer."

"While talking to some lady in a bar?"

"I'm on a break."

I heard the big ape sigh. "So you won't save us both a lot of trouble and come clean?"

"I don't have anything else to say right now, Gordo, sorry. As soon as I do you'll be the first to know, I promise. Look, I want to get back to my drink and the blonde, okay?"

I disconnected without waiting for a reply. Take that, Gordo! I was feeling very much the big strong man as I walked back toward Irene, who was watching me intently.

"It was my man on the force calling me with an update," I said as I took my seat.

"The police force?" she asked, impressed.

"Yeah. A P.I. needs his informants."

"Wow. You really are something, aren't you?"

"Well . . . I don't know about that. I am just a man doing his job, that's all."

It was at that moment that a voice behind me pulled me from Irene's green eyes.

"Derek Lasker?"

I turned and saw two somber men in police uniforms. One of them was in his fifties and the younger man had a thin ugly brown moustache.

"Yeah?"

The older man said, "Come with us."

"I'm . . . I'm in the middle of something here and—"

He grabbed my arm and nearly pulled me off the stool. "We aren't asking. We're telling."

"Is everything okay?" Irene asked.

"Sure," I said with a weak smile. "This is just the way we do business, you know, for appearances sake."

The man started pulling me away when the mustached one said, "Aren't you gonna to be a gentleman and pay the bill before you go? Not going to stiff her with it, are you?"

"No, no, of course not." I pulled out my wallet.

Officer Moustache nudged the older cop and said, "I wouldn't mind stiffing her . . ."

I tossed $30 on the bar wishing I had the guts to make him apologize for the comment.

"Nice meeting you, Irene," I said as they pulled me away. Should I have called out and asked for her number? Would that be improper to do while being led away by two cops?

She watched me go with worry lines across her forehead. Was she wondering whether I was just another pig tossing lies at her hoping to win her favor?

But before the two cops had me out the door, she turned to the bartender and ordered another vodka and cranberry.

Chapter 16

They held open the back door of a squad car and drove me to 43 Division on Lawrence Avenue East, a few kilometers east of Winston Churchill Collegiate.

"What's this about?"

"You'll see," said Officer Moustache from behind the wheel.

"Don't you have to read me my rights?"

The older detective turned and looked at me through the Plexiglas dividing the front and back seats. "Did you do something that makes you think we should arrest you?"

"No."

"Then just keep your mouth shut and all will become clear."

Though I would have loved to rant and rave about how my taxes pay their wages and that I deserve to be treated with respect, I kept my mouth closed until they pulled in behind 43 Division. The older man held open the door and he motioned for me to enter the building.

They led me toward an interview room, or should I call it an interrogation room, and Officer Moustache opened the door and pointed at a chair on one side of the table.

"Sit and wait," he said.

What else could I do except do as I was told? I sat in the metal chair for the next twenty minutes and my anxiety level increased with each passing second. What was I doing there? Was this Gordon Grossman's idea? Was he trying to strong-arm me into giving up the name of Bob Junior? I had almost convinced myself that I would do just that—that I would tell him everything I knew about the kid if they would stop treating me like a criminal—when the door opened and a man in a suit walked in carrying a file folder. He looked familiar and I thought he may have been present in the English classroom that morning.

He sat down across from me and stared at me.

He didn't say a word.

"Are you going to say something?" I asked, my nerves frayed to the point of breaking.

"Don't you have anything to say for yourself?"

"What the hell do you mean by that? I've been sitting here for twenty minutes and I don't even know why I was brought here!"

"Is that a fact?"

"Of course it is!" His passionless face was making me all the angrier. "Why are you playing games with me? What am I doing here? Am I under arrest? I haven't done anything!"

"We're not so sure about that."

"What? What do you think I've done?"

"It's not a question of what we think you've done, but what we know you've done."

This exchange was going to drive me insane.

"This is like something out of Kafka . . ." Or perhaps a dark play by Beckett. I took a deep breath in an attempt to calm down. My heart was beating much too quickly, and even though I knew I hadn't done anything illegal, I probably looked guilty to the suited bastard sitting across from me. Like I said before, being around cops could make anyone feel guilty, so surely being left alone in an interrogation cell without being told why you were there was enough to make even the calmest and most collected person feel like someone at the top of the most wanted list.

"Okay," I began, ". . . enough of your theatrics, okay? How about you just lay it out and tell me what I'm doing here and we can talk about it. Whatever is bothering you can

be resolved. I'm sure that this is all just a big misunderstanding."

"I don't think so, Mr. Lasker. And it isn't up to you to
decide what goes on in this room. It isn't your place to tell
me what to do. If I want to continue with these theatrics, I
will and there's not a damned thing you can do about it."

"Oh I get it. Is another cop going to come in and he'll be
nice to me? Is that it? Isn't the 'good' cop-bad cop' thing a
bit of a cliché? Doesn't the force have any new techniques?"

"There is no one else, Mr. Lasker. Just me and you."

He was in his mid-forties, a little heavy and meaty like
a retired boxer. His hair was once brown but was almost
entirely grey. His eyes were dark and intense and the way
they were staring at me was increasing my nervousness.

"Lucky me," I said.

What was I doing there? Why wouldn't he tell me?

He smiled. "That's right. Lucky you." Then again he just
sat there and stared at me.

"Look . . . if I am not being charged, there's no reason I
can't walk out this door."

"That's true."

"Listen, I have a friend on the force and if you could call
him I am sure that he—"

"You're talking about Gordon Grossman?"

"That's right."

"He won't help you. He knows you're here. You had your
chance to talk to him. I believe he called you before you
were picked up?"

"Ohhh . . . so that's what this is all about. You want me
to tell you what I know about the cat."

"What do you know about it?"

I brought my hands together. "Finally! He asks me a
question!"

"No need to be a smartass, Mr. Lasker."

"I think that this whole situation requires that I be a complete smartass, Mr. Whoever-You-Are. I would call you by your name, but I noticed that you never bothered giving it to me."

"Very perceptive of you. And it's Detective Whoever-You-Are, not mister."

"Oh excuse me for the insult."

"Are you getting angry with me, Mr. Lasker?"

"Of course I am! This whole situation is absurd!"

"Is it?"

"Yes!"

"You seem to be avoiding talking about the cat."

"I'm not avoiding it! I was just thanking you for finally asking me a genuine question instead of sitting there like something out of George Orwell."

"You consider yourself pretty smart, don't you?"

"What do you mean?"

"First you say that this situation is like Kafka, and then you say it's like Orwell. So which is it?"

"I don't know . . . both."

"Do you always try to make people think you're smart?"

"Another question! How wonderful!"

"I've now asked you two questions and you've yet to give an answer."

"You asked three questions. I answered you and said that this situation is both like Kafka and Orwell."

The detective's eyes bore into me and I felt proud of myself, even though I had no reason to. Was I really concerned with scoring points against this man? Shouldn't I have been more concerned about getting out of the police station?

"Yes, yes, you are very clever. Good for you." He stood and walked to the door and stopped when he had his hand on the knob. "You keep thinking of smart things to say and we can talk more later."

He left the room and once again I was alone.

Chapter 17

You know the old saying.

You don't own beer, you only rent it.

Moments after the no-name detective closed the door, my bladder suddenly made itself known. It always happened that way with beer and me: I'd feel fine and then the moment I needed to urinate the feeling went quickly from awareness to urgency.

I tried the door handle. Locked. I was free to go and yet the door was locked?

"Hey!" I yelled. I pounded on the door for good measure. "Hey! I need to use the bathroom! Hey!" I continued to bang on the door and scream while my need increased exponentially. I knew that if I was left in that room for much longer I was going to have little choice but to pick a corner and go.

I was saved from that unpleasant option by the opening of the door. A uniformed officer stood there staring at me.

"What are you yelling about in here?"

"I need to piss something fierce!"

He looked completely unimpressed and pointed to a door that, thankfully, was close, and I dashed toward it.

Ahhh. I am sure there is no need to describe the glorious feeling of going when the need is so great.

As I turned to wash my hands, I noticed that my entire outlook had changed. Gone was the anxiety. I hadn't done anything wrong and I had nothing to fear. If they thought I had done something wrong I would curb my aggressive behavior and answer any questions without hesitation or smart-ass remarks. The only question was whether I should give up Bob Junior. If I told them all I knew about him would it be enough to collect my $10,000? After all, the radio announcement clearly stated that the reward came only after the successful prosecution of the guilty party. And did I trust the cops to even find enough evidence to convict Bob Junior? I was hoping to gift wrap the case, and in so doing, revitalize my career. I had visions of making the front page shaking the hand of the Chief of Police. Perhaps it was time to think smaller and let the cops take over and trust them to complete the investigation.

The uniformed cop had come in the bathroom with me (standard procedure I supposed) so I asked him, "What's the name of the detective who I was speaking to?"

"He didn't tell you?"

"Nope."

"And you think I will?"

"Why not," I smiled, "Be a sport."

The cop walked up to me, grabbed me by the front of my shirt, pulling out several chest-hairs in the process, and got close enough to me that I could smell his foul breath.

"Listen you goddamned pervert. I would like nothing better than to toss you around this room right now, so don't you push your goddamned luck." He shoved me as he let go and I stumbled backward and nearly fell. "Now get back to your room before I lose my temper."

The look on the man's face told me to keep my mouth shut and I ever-so-meekly walked down the hall and back into the familiar interrogation room. I jumped as the cop slammed the door behind me.

The good feeling I had after relieving myself was gone.

Pervert? Me?

I was all the more confused.

Perhaps this whole episode had nothing to do with Mittens.

I sat down and closed my eyes and did my best to relax.

The detective had told me that I could leave but I didn't

believe him. The locked door was solid evidence of that. I had the feeling that whatever made them so angry at me was not going to allow them to graciously let me walk out the door and spend the rest of my night trying to track down the lovely Irene Johansen. It was almost 9:00 so if nothing else, this surprising incarceration had kept me from having to decide if "John Sherman" was going to learn some knife-fighting techniques from Bob Junior.

Everything about this case had me feeling like I was just seeing the tip of the iceberg poking out of the frozen sea.

A half hour later, the door opened again and in walked the no-name detective followed by the old Lieutenant who'd lost his cool that morning and let slip about the human tongue in Mitten's mouth. The two men stood in the doorway and stared down at me.

"You're in a lot of trouble," the Lieutenant said.

"Will someone please tell me why?" I asked.

"See? What did I tell you? The guy is a complete smart-ass."

"Did he ask for a lawyer?"

"No."

"I need a lawyer?"

"That's for you to decide," said the Lieutenant. "I think it's time you come clean before we take your whole world apart, understand?"

"I am ready to talk," I said. "My only concern is about the $10,000."

No-name shook his head. "So he did it for the money. Pathetic."

"People will do anything for money. You work this job as long as I have and you'll learn that people will sink to the lowest depths in order to get a few lousy dollars."

No-name added, "Judging by the look of that motel, he needs every cent he can get."

"You went to the motel?"

"Of course we did. You're way behind in the rent."

"You talked to Hasid?"

"Is that his name? I asked him if you ever made improper advances toward any of his daughters, who were there and looked pretty cute, and he said he didn't think so."

That really pissed me off, and I sprang to my feet. "Why the hell would you ask him something like that?"

"We have your car, Mr. Lasker . . ." the Lieutenant said. "Just show him the photo, Mike."

Detective Mike opened his file and tossed and 8x10 picture onto the table. It was my Corolla, with me plainly visible, taking photos with my digital camera.

"The way we see it," Mike said, "Only a pervert parks outside of a high school and snaps pictures of students as they leave. We've been trying to figure out what you're trying to say with the cat's head and our psychologists have come up with some pretty twisted theories."

"Now why don't you tell us everything," Lieutenant said, "so we can wrap up this case and I can go home and watch the last few innings of the ball game."

Chapter 18

I was stunned by this turn of events.

It was made all the more strange by Lieutenant Hendrickson, who in spite of his eagerness to achieve a speedy conclusion to this case, continued to ramble on about baseball.

"Did I ever tell you that I was at the first home game the Jays played out at old Exhibition Stadium on April 7th, 1977? Anne Murray sang the national anthem and I used to think she was a sexy woman and now I hear she left her husband to live with a woman. Shame that such a fine looking lady decides to go that way. It was a great game too. Doug Ault hit two home runs then ended up shooting himself dead when he was fifty-four. Ault was something that cold April day and maybe it was hard for the poor fella that the rest of his career didn't go the way things did on that opening day. They beat the White Sox 9-5. Helluva game baseball is. And tonight they're playing the Yankees, and I hate them more than any other team, even more than the Oakland A's, so how about you tell the Detective what the hell you were doing at the school taking pictures of kids. What kind of pervert does a thing like that anyway?"

"Why don't you leave this to me and I'll let you know what he has to say, alright?" Mike suggested.

The Lieutenant nodded. "Okay then. Just nail this bastard to the wall so we can get the press off my back, understand?"

"But I'm not your man," I said.

"I say you are," was the Lieutenant's reply as he left the room.

Mike took the seat on the other side of the table. "Okay, smart guy, are you feeling more like talking than you were earlier?"

"Definitely. This is all a big misunderstanding and I want to clear it up. I'm on your side!"

"Uh huh. Right. I'm sure you'll understand if I'm skeptical. So tell me what you were doing at the school yesterday afternoon."

I took a deep breath. If telling all cost me the $10,000, so be it. I wanted to end all suspicion as soon as possible.

"I was on a case. I'm a private investigator hired by a man to watch his son."

"Watch his son?"

"I'm telling you the truth. His name is Bob Linehan Senior and he hired me to follow his son because Bob Junior has been hanging out with a rough crowd. Linehan wanted to make sure his kid didn't get into any serious trouble."

"You said you were working for this Linehan. Does that mean you're not working for him anymore?"

"No."

"You got a P.I. license?"

"Yeah." I pulled out my wallet and showed it to him. He wrote down the number.

"How about giving me Linehan's phone number?"

I looked it up on my cell phone and gave it to him.

"How long were you working for him?"

"Two days."

"That's it?"

"Yeah. He decided, after talking to his wife, that he felt wrong about hiring someone to tail his kid. If you ask me, tailing him was a good idea since I got the feeling Bob Junior was up to no good."

"Okay. Let's say you really were on a case and that this license is genuine—"

"It is."

"It still doesn't explain why you were taking pictures of kids outside of the school."

"I wasn't taking pictures of kids! God! You make it sound so seamy. I was taking pictures of Bob Junior and his friends. I was surveilling them and I wanted to keep a record. C'mon, it wasn't like I was snapping pictures in the girl's change room or anything."

"You think this is funny?"

"Definitely not."

"So you say he hired you to follow his kid because he was hanging out with a rough crowd?"

"Yeah. He said his wife was afraid of these new friends because they looked like gang members. He did that thing . . . you know . . . where someone says 'I don't want to sound prejudiced' then says something complete prejudiced?"

"This Bob Linehan is a racist?"

"I don't know about that . . . but he seemed to be awfully worried about his son hanging out with black kids. I mean . . . he lives in Scarborough, what does he expect?"

"Do you have a problem with black people?"

"Of course not."

"Tell me about the cat."

I sighed. "Okay. I think the cat head in front of Winston Collegiate belongs to Bob Linehan's neighbor. He hired me because he got freaked out when he found a headless cat in his backyard. He thought his son Bob Junior might have done it."

"Why'd he think that his son did it?"

"He seemed to know that the cat was there and he has a thing for knives. Apparently, he has a closet full of them and he teaches classes on knife-fighting techniques."

The detective jotted down this information.

"I was staking out their house when I heard about the cat head and since it was put in front of Bob Junior's school I figured it seemed likely that he might have had something to do with it. So I went up to the school, which was where I ran into Gord Grossman and the Lieutenant, who seems a bit short of a full load, if you know what I mean."

"The Lieutenant has done more for this city than you will ever do so don't you say a word about him."

"Okay okay."

Again the silent treatment.

"So what now?" I asked. "I thought you'd be pleased to hear all of this."

He shrugged. "It all sounds like bullshit to me, that's all." He reaches out for my cell phone that was on the table. "Mind if I take this for a minute?"

"If it will help clear up this mess, no, please take it."

He stood. "I am going to go make a couple calls and maybe that will give some answers. You need anything?"

"Some water or coffee? I've been in here for a long time without anything."

"Okay. I'll see what I can do." He walked to the door. "Sit tight."

"Like I have a choice."

"You can leave anytime you want."

He said that, yet when he closed the door it locked behind him. My mouth was feeling very dry and the suggestion of a drink made me all the more aware of my thirst. Was it the buzzing fluorescent lamp that was causing my headache? Stress must have been a contributing factor, as well as the lack of food. I had eaten very little that day, other than a few french fries at the bar.

I needed to get out of there.

I'd lose my mind if I was kept locked up for much longer.

Ten minutes later Detective Mike returned without anything for me to drink. He tossed his file folder to the table and looked down at me like I was a piece of garbage.

"Guess what?" he asked. "I just found out that you're a liar."

"What do you mean?"

"Bob Linehan says he never heard of you and that he's never hired a detective in his life."

Chapter 19

"He's lying!"

Mike smiled. "Someone is."

"Don't you see what he's doing? He's protecting his son! Linehan told me he buried the cat in his backyard to hide the evidence! Go dig it up and that will prove—"

"We're not digging up anyone's yard."

I thought a moment. "My cell phone . . . check the incoming and outgoing calls and you'll see that I had several conversations with Bob Linehan. The first one was yesterday . . . early afternoon."

"The first one was yesterday? I thought you said you worked for him for two days. Your story is already unraveling, isn't it?"

"I billed him for two days and he paid up since I think he wanted to see the last of me after the cat head turned up. He knew it was Mittens. He told me so. He said, 'How many cat heads do you think are out there?' He was freaking out. Now that this is escalating, he doesn't want any attention brought to his son. When he paid me this morning he even suggested that someone might have planted the cat in his backyard in order to frame his son."

"Do you realize how far-fetched all of this is sounding?"

"Look, you have me sitting here when I could be out there helping to crack this case."

Mike laughed. "Crack the case! Listen to you talking like a real detective! Your license is expired, did you know that?"

"No, I didn't."

"Didn't pay your annual fee. Judging by those track marks on your arms I know where your money is going."

"These are from work I did at a pharmaceutical company! I told that to Gord Grossman!"

"More tall tales. You stink to high heaven for all this, Lasker. And I'm going to nail you for it."

My anger and frustration was rising again. "What, so you can get the Lieutenant home in time for the last few innings?"

He slammed his hand down on the table. "I told you to shut up about him!"

The door opened as the huge form of Gordon Grossman entered. "Mike, let me talk to him for a minute."

"This isn't an ETF matter, Grossman."

"I went to high school with this guy. Maybe he'll talk to me."

"You had him and you let him walk out of the school and now you want me to hand him over to you? Don't you have any doors to kick in? Any suspects to blow away?"

"C'mon, Mike, relax. No need to get pissy. I'm not here to steal your thunder. I just wanna to talk to him and clear this up as much as you do."

Mike stood and shrugged. "Knock yourself out, cowboy."

The detective slammed the door behind him leaving my former friend and me alone in the room.

"Gordo! Am I glad to see you! They think I had something to do with this!"

"I know they do, and I wonder if they're right . . ."

"What? You know me better than that! Chopping the head off a cat and sticking it on a post in front of a high school? You really think that's something I am capable of?"

He shrugged. "Who knows? I haven't known you for years. You don't seem like the man I once knew. The old Lasky would've been screaming bloody murder about being caged up like this."

"You think I haven't been pissed off? I'm trying to keep my cool and answer all of Mike's questions so I can get the hell out of here."

"He told you that this Linehan denies knowing you?"

"Yeah. Did anyone check my phone and see that I have incoming and outgoing calls from his number?"

"We did. Look, for what it's worth, I believe you. I don't know why. Maybe it's because we won a lot of championships together years ago. Maybe that's softened my judgment, or maybe I know you better than the other guys in here. Besides, I said you were okay this morning, so now if you turn out to be the perp I end up looking bad and I won't stand for that."

"I can help you find out who's behind all this, but not while I am locked up in here."

"Will you be straight with me and tell me the whole story so I don't look like a damn fool?"

"Okay."

I retold the story I told Mike but added my suspicions about Bob Junior and Ray and that there was something there that seemed fishy and was worthy of more digging.

"I already talked to them and they think I'm a security specialist. They trust me, at least a little, and if you give me a little time and I can hand you this whole case wrapped up like a birthday present. I know that Bob Linehan Junior cut the head off the cat but I have no idea whether he put the head in front of the school, though I think he did. I don't know whose tongue is in its mouth. With a little time I think I can find out, and then you can make the arrest and I can collect the reward."

Gordon stared at me with his arms crossed over his broad chest. "Do you realize that the powers-that-be make you for this?"

"The dotty Lieutenant said as much after a lengthy exegesis on Blue Jays history." I held up my hands. "Sorry.

I know I shouldn't make fun of him."

"I don't care. He is an old fool and way past retirement. He's an embarrassment to the force."

"Don't let Mike hear you talk like that."

He smiled. "I can take care of Mike."

"I'm sure you can." I suspected that Gordo could take care of an angry grizzly.

"I'm going to go out on a limb here, Lasky, and cut you loose. I want this case wrapped up fast and would like nothing better than to drag the bastards in by their hair in front of all the news cameras. I looked through your car and saw your bugs and tracers and all the sort of gizmos that I would love to use but can't because I need to get a warrant to do so. I will let you walk out of here, but only if you agree to work with me and to keep me informed every step of the way. In return, I'll be there for you. You need any sort of information I can pull from our computers or if you need some muscle, or whatever, you call me and I'll be there. All you need to do is to work your ass off and dig up some solid leads. Does that sound like a deal?"

I was so relieved to hear his words that I could feel tears begin to well up. I forced them away so Gordo wouldn't think I was a complete sissy. "That sounds perfect."

"I get the glory and you get the cash. Win-win. But Lasky, I need you to understand something. If you screw me on this and I find out that you had something to do with this cat head, I will be very, very pissed off. And you remember what I used to do to people who pissed me off?"

I just nodded since his stern look froze any words from coming forth.

"Now imagine what I can do now that I have the full force of the law behind me. I can kill legally, you know that. All it takes is to toss a weapon near your dead body and to tell those pricks at SIU that you were going to use it and I get to walk. You hear what I am saying?"

How could I miss it? I nodded again.

"Say it."

"Screw you and die."

He smiled his predator's smile.

"You do understand." He held open the door. "Happy hunting."

Chapter 20

I needed a cigarette.

No. I needed many cigarettes.

Cigarettes and a big bottle of malt liquor would help calm my frazzled nerves. I thought I had half a pack of smokes in my car that was parked somewhere on the back lot but I needed Gordo to bring me my keys and unlock the gate.

I waited outside, pacing back and forth and for the entire time I wondered if this was some kind of sick game and Gordo, Mike, or even the old Lieutenant, would walk out the door and put me in handcuffs and lead me back inside laughing like demons. Thankfully Gordo walked out and handed me my phone and keys and seemed to have no malicious intent. He punched in a code on the keypad and the large gate whirred open.

"Your car is back there somewhere."

"I'll find it," I said as I walked away.

"Call me soon, Lasky. I want hourly updates."

"You'll have them. But listen, it's 10:00. I'm not sure what I am going to be able to do tonight . . ."

"Do something, Lasky." The gate was closing between us. "We need results double quick. Put your nose to the grindstone. No time for fooling around. No time for drinking or talking to pretty blondes or for shooting smack, okay?"

I nearly started to argue that I never shot smack but realized it was pointless. Instead I just nodded and said, "Okay, I'll get to work."

My car was nearby, and it felt good to slip behind the wheel. I did indeed find half a pack of cigarettes there. My hands shook as I lit one. God, it felt good to inhale. I felt a lot of weight fall from my shoulders as I breathed out the smoke. I did a quick inventory and thought that all my things were still inside. I wasn't sure about the legality of my tracers and bugs so I was thankful that there were not seized.

I started my car and backed out. Again came a moment of anxiety as I waited for the chain-link fence to open, but the sensors finally kicked in and it slowly shuddered open. I pulled out slowly and was thrilled to get away from terrible 43 Division. I had little doubt that the place would feature prominently in future nightmares.

Gordo wanted me to get to work but there was no way I could do so before washing the grimy feeling from my skin. I had been treated like a piece of garbage for so many hours that I was beginning to feel like one. It had been a long miserable day (the sweet Irene interlude felt like a distant memory) and perhaps after a hot shower, a bite to eat and a quick drink I would feel capable of shadowing Bob Junior.

I was in for a surprise when I pulled into the motel and climbed the stairs to my room.

The doorknob was covered in yellow tape and there was a hand-written notice on the door saying I needed to go the office. This couldn't be good.

Hasid was working the desk and he was not pleased to see me.

"I want you out!" he said sharply.

"Why?"

"Police come here and ask questions about you! About whether you ever touch my daughters! My daughters, Lasker! I do not want you here any longer! Here!" He tossed a suitcase onto the counter. "I already pack your things. Get out."

"This isn't my bag."

"I give it to you. Just leave and you don't have to pay

your bill. Just leave before I call the police. He left me a card and said to call if you give any trouble. I call him right now if you don't leave!"

I shook my head. That damned Detective Mike. "This is all a big misunderstanding, Hasid. They didn't—,"

He shook a finger in my face. "With my daughters, I do not take chances! Leave now and never return."

What could I say to him? Arguing my case would only make him more upset. Though I hated to have the kind man thinking that I was some sort of pervert, the only decent thing I could do was honor his wishes and leave. I pulled the suitcase from the counter.

"Thanks for everything, Hasid." I walked out without another word, a feeling of sadness nearly overwhelming me.

And just like that, I had become homeless.

Chapter 21

I wanted to curl up in a ball and feel sorry for myself.

I wanted to drink a hundred bottles of beer and smoke a million cigarettes.

I wanted to take inventory of my life and catalog every instance where I screwed up. To think of every poor decision, and trust me there have been many, and curse my stupidity and weakness for getting me into this predicament.

I had been a good student!

I had been a good athlete!

I had been smart and ambitious!

I could have done so much with my life!

Enough! I cut off these thoughts by imagining what Gordon Grossman would say to me: 'Just get to work, crybaby!' or something equally motivational.

I took stock of my current state of affairs: I had nowhere to live, a quarter tank of gas, a twenty year old Corolla, some electronic surveillance equipment, a vinyl suitcase full of dirty clothes, and $20 to my name. Not a terribly impressive list of assets after close to forty years on the planet. I would have considered this rock bottom if it were not for the case. There was still that faint glimmer of hope. If only I could pull enough information together to convince the cops that Bob Junior was their man, not me, then I would have $10,000 to my name and could start my life all over again.

It felt very pagan to think that a cat head with a human tongue might prove to be my only salvation.

I pulled out of the motel (Hasid did not look up from his desk as I went past) and drove a block to a convenience store, where I purchased some food and drink in case this turned into a long night. The bill came to $11 leaving me with a $5 bill and a pocket full of change. Rock bottom was getting closer.

I clicked on my tracker and followed the signal to Ray's dojo. It was not quite 11:00 p.m. Class might still be in session. What to do now?

Since Bob Senior has disavowed knowing me, I had to assume that he saw the danger I could bring to his family. To protect his son, he could have told Bob Juniorabout me. He could have made up something or another. He could have told him I was a cop. I had no way of knowing if my cover was blown, so I decided to keep John Sherman under wraps and go back to watching Bob from a distance. I liked this plan. I felt far too overwhelmed by the events of the day to start playing the undercover game.

Though I parked across the street from the dojo as far away from a streetlight as I could get, I still felt exposed. In the old days when I was working for the insurance companies I would have rented another car to avoid the suspect spotting me but with $5 to my name that was out of the question. I would just have to keep my distance and hope I was lucky.

I drank the lousy burnt coffee (it was a huge Styrofoam cup for 75 cents so what did I expect?) and ate some beef jerky and peanuts and began to feel better as the caffeine, salt and, calories kicked in. I would have loved to buy some cigarettes but the thought of spending my last dollars on cancer sticks was depressing.

Just before midnight there was some movement at the front door and people began to file out. Most looked young, somewhere around Bob Junior's age, with a few older men tossed in. They all seemed quite rowdy, as if the late-night lesson had charged them with aggression and adrenaline. I guess a good knife-fighting class will do that. The three older men (aged mid-thirties or so) made their way to their vehicles while the younger guys stayed outside the dojo, horsing around, sparring and acting like your average hyperactive teenage boys. I kept watch with my binoculars and saw Bob Junior exit with Ray. The crowd greeted Bob Junior enthusiastically while Ray locked the front door.

They stood around chatting and I wished I had the courage to pull closer to get within range of my parabolic mic. After a few minutes they got into their cars and pulled out like a convoy with Bob Junior and Ray leading the way in the orange Civic.

I called Gordo.

"Hey, Lasky."

"You said I could call you for help or info."

"That's right."

"There's a guy that I'd love to know more about. Runs a martial arts gym off of Kingston Road."

"What's the link?"

"Bob Linehan Junior teaches knife fighting there."

"Nice. Okay. What's the name?"

"Ray."

"Ray? No last name?"

"I don't know it." I gave him the address of the dojo. "You should be able to find him with that. He says he's former US Marine, but who knows if that's true."

"I'll see what I can dig up."

"Listen, let me ask you a hypothetical question. Let's say an honest citizen were to find themselves in someone else's home or business, let's say they slipped in through an open window, and they found evidence of a crime and called you boys in blue. Would you be able to use what that person found?"

Gordo laughed. "I knew letting you loose was the right thing to do, Lasky. If this honest citizen were to find something and call in a tip then all we would have to do is cook up some probable cause to get into the premises all nice and legal."

"Good. Thanks for feeding my curious mind."

"Go get 'em, tiger."

I tossed the phone to the seat and finished my now cold coffee.

Once Ray, Bob Junior and the others had been gone for ten minutes I took my bag of tricks and walked to the dojo.

Some of my skills were rusty, but I am proud to say I picked the lock in twenty seconds flat. I stepped inside and locked it behind me. I hadn't spotted an alarm on my previous visit so I walked up the stairs casually.

I had that special high that one gets from committing a felony. Crime may not pay, but it can make you feel like a million bucks!

Chapter 22

The dojo was bright enough thanks to light coming through the several windows. It never got very dark anywhere in the Greater Toronto Area. The few times I'd gotten away from the city and spent time in the great outdoors, the true darkness of night amazed me. It was incredible not being able to see your hand in front of your face. In the dojo, I didn't even need my flashlight.

I didn't really know what I was looking for. Maybe I was just being nosey. Maybe I just needed to do something to keep Gordo off my back. I pulled out my cell and set it to silent mode in case he called back. I was alone in the place but one can never be too careful when committing a B & E that could cost six months in jail.

I went into the office where I had spoken with Bob Junior the day before. It was a windowless room so I pulled out my Scorpion flashlight and took a closer look at the photos on the wall. They did have someone in them who looked like Ray (it was hard to tell with the hat and sunglasses), wearing camouflage and smiling with a group of similarly dressed men. No way to tell if these were Marines or just guys dressed as such. Near the photo was a medal in a frame. It looked like a purple heart, though I couldn't be sure since I'd only seen one in the movies. There was nothing in the frame to indicate to whom it was awarded or for what. I'd seen enough war movies to know they were awarded to soldiers wounded in battle, but I had no way of knowing whether it was given to Ray, or even if it was genuine. I didn't think a photo of it would be of any use but just the same I used my digital camera to snap a picture of everything on the wall.

There was a small desk against the back wall. I slipped on a pair of latex gloves to be sure I didn't leave fingerprints behind and then went through the drawers. I found nothing interesting until I discovered that the bottom right drawer was locked. That had my alarm bells ringing. I was again impressed with my skills with the pick and torsion wrench as I popped the lock in seconds.

Inside was a neat row of ten DVDs with dates written on them, spanning the past year. Nothing else was in the drawer.

What was on them that warranted a lock?

They could have been something dull like classes or training exercises but my instincts whispered no. I debated for a brief moment but then tucked one of the DVDs into my bag.

There was nothing else of interest in the office so I moved to the room next door. It was a storage room that held assorted equipment. There were gloves, padded helmets and other protective gear one wears during sparring, as well as wooden swords shaped like the ones samurai used. There were pads that people put on their hands to use as targets for fighters practicing punches or kicks. I spun my flashlight and saw a large red wooden wardrobe that looked like the fake Chinese crap you can buy in any low-end furniture store. Must have been close to six feet across. It had a lock on it that quickly fell to my skills. I was feeling much better about myself now. I wasn't proving to be much of a P.I. but my criminal skills were strong. Admittedly, it was a somewhat depressing thought.

As I opened the wardrobe I was met with the smell of spicy incense. Inside were swords and knives of various shapes and sizes mounted on the inner doors. I panned my light to the right and jumped when I saw the figure that dominated the cabinet.

It was not a Buddha, or some other Eastern deity you might expect to see in a martial arts dojo. Instead it was an ancient-looking drawing of a crossed-legged figure sitting on a pillar. It had a man's body, black feathered wings, and a goat's head with long black horns. Its right hand was pointed upward at a white crescent moon and the left pointed downward at a black crescent moon. On its forehead was a five-pointed star. I didn't know much about religion, but I knew that was a picture of Satan and the cabinet was some sort of shrine. I took pictures of everything inside, feeling very freaked out as I did.

What the hell did this mean?

Was Ray a Satanist?

Were there really such people?

My heart was beating quickly as I closed the cabinet. I wanted to get out of there and process everything I'd found. I didn't know what the shrine meant and I did not want to stick around and find out. To be cautious I looked out the window to make sure that Ray hadn't returned and the coast looked clear. It would have been like something out of a horror movie: finding a creepy shrine to the devil and then turning around to find Ray standing there saying, 'I see you have discovered my little secret.' Then he would rip out my heart and eat it. OK, I was freaking myself out. I needed to get out of there. I crept down the stairs and after taking another look I let myself out.

It took me a few minutes to relock the door since I was shaken by my dark discovery. The longer it took, the more my anxiety grew. I kept turning my head, imagining that Ray or Bob Junior was suddenly going to appear behind me with curved knives in their hands and evil smiles on their faces. I had to fight the urge to take off without re-engaging the lock. It finally clicked and I jogged to my Corolla. I hopped in, my face wet with perspiration, and roared away from the dojo as quickly as the old car would take me.

Chapter 23

I called Gordo again first thing the next morning. I had left messages the night before.

I'd spent a restless night in the backseat of my car in a parking lot behind a Shopper's Drug Mart. It took me a long time to fall asleep even though it had been an exhausting day. Something about that drawing stuck in my mind. Something about the way I had turned my flashlight and found it suddenly. The eyes of the Beast seemed to look right into my soul. Every time I closed my eyes I could see them. Several times I reached over the front seat to click on the radio to banish the dark images. I didn't know what time I managed to fall asleep and I doubted I got more than a few hours.

They mentioned the cat head on news radio that morning and said that there were no reports of suspects, but that the police were chasing every lead.

But I knew this wasn't true.

I gave them Bob Junior and they didn't want him! All it took to scare them off was the line Bob Senior gave them. I was tempted to call him and ask him outright why he lied to the cops, but I didn't. It wasn't the right time, though it could come to that.

Gordon sounded tired.

"Yeah?"

"It's Lasker."

"You know how early it is?"

"Yeah. Did I wake you up?"

"Almost. Alarm just went off."

"How about we meet up and you buy me breakfast."

"You got something to tell me? Did you snoop up anything good?"

I thought of the goat-headed man. "Maybe."
We set the place and agreed to meet in an hour.

I could have told Gord what I'd discovered the previous night without meeting him, though that would have meant going without breakfast.

I beat him to the restaurant and I wanted to use the washroom to clean up. I was feeling particularly grimy and the waitress looked at me with suspicion as I walked in.

"Washroom's are for customers only," she said.

"I'm a customer. I need a table for two." If I wouldn't have looked so rough I might have snapped at her. As it was there was no way I could blame her. Not only was I homeless, I was beginning to look homeless.

I did the best I could in the small sink. I used a few meters of paper towel to give myself a good scrubbing.

I slid into a table and motioned for some coffee. I loaded it with cream and sugar and drained it quickly. When she brought back the pot for a refill I asked for some toast.

"To tide me over while I wait for my friend." She looked at me skeptically so I added, "He's a cop." She shrugged and told the cook to pop in an order of white toast.

I had finished both slices (with peanut butter and strawberry jam) by the time Gordon entered. The big man waved for a coffee as he slid into the booth across from me.

"So you had a productive night?"

"I found some interesting things."

The waitress returned with Gord's coffee and I ordered the lumberjack breakfast: three eggs, two pancakes, bacon, sausage, ham, homefries and toast. "And a glass of orange juice," I added.

"Christ, Lasky, you got a hunger this morning." He turned to the waitress. "Just the coffee for me, darlin'. So what have you dug up?"

"I'll show you." I pulled out my camera and forwarded the viewer until I found the chilling image I had found in the wardrobe. I handed him the camera and he looked at it.

"What's this supposed to be? Goat boy?"

"It's the devil."

"So?"

"It was the centerpiece in a creepy little shrine our man Ray has in his martial arts dojo alongside a bunch of swords and knives."

"A satanic martial arts instructor? That's what you're bringing me?"

"Doesn't this set off bells for you? You got a mutilated cat on a stick with a tongue in the mouth. You don't think that a crime like that has some dark undertones? Satanic even?"

"Christ, Lasky, if I started to think that everyone who committed the evil shit I see every day was satanic I would start thinking that the whole damned city was in a coven or something."

"Did you find out anything about this Ray character?"

"Not yet. Today."

"I have a picture if that would help."

"Not really."

"I also have this." I held up the DVD.

"You burned me a copy of Madonna's greatest hits?"

"I took it from the dojo. It's a DVD. He had a whole row of them in a locked drawer in his desk."

The waitress set down my enormous plate of food and a smaller plate for the second order of toast. I immediately tucked in.

"So you stole part of this guy's porno collection, so what."

"Worth looking at, don't you think?"

"Have you watched it?"

"Nope. I don't have a player."

He stood with the disk in hand. "I have my laptop in the cruiser. I'll go check it out and be back. God, you eat like you haven't seen food in a week, you know that?"

"My mama always said a boy should have a healthy appetite."

"Yeah? Seems you got that and them some."

I was on my forth cup of coffee and was mopping up the last of the yolk with my final triangle of toast when Gordo came back. He tossed the DVD onto the table.

"There's a lock on it. I can't play it without entering a six-digit code."

"That doesn't make any alarm bells ring? A locked DVD hidden in a locked drawer?"

"Maybe it's some majorly kinky porn."

I smiled. "Even if that is the case, doesn't that make you want to crack it and see what's inside all the more?"

"You got me there, Lasky. I am a little curious. I got a guy who knows about computers. You might as well ride with me. That is if you're done stuffing your face."

I patted my stomach. "For now."

Chapter 24

Since Gord was paying, I ordered a coffee to go. Being homeless and sleeping in the back of my car with no means of support, I wondered if taking handouts was something I was going to have to become accustomed to. A cheery thought for so early in the morning! I sipped the sweet coffee as we drove west toward the heart of Toronto.

We were roaring down the streets in a huge police Suburban, swerving into oncoming lanes and putting on the siren to blast through red lights. Gordo had The Tragically Hip turned up to a near-painful volume on the stereo. *New Orleans is sinking and I don't wanna swim.* I don't know if the loud music and erratic driving was for my benefit or was simply the way the reckless maniac always drove. We didn't exchange a word during the twenty minute trip (it would have been at least forty minutes for those driving without the protection of a badge) and we pulled up in front of a rundown computer store on River Street between Queen Street and Dundas Avenue. That was the name of the place: Computer Store. It said so on the sign hanging above the door of what appeared to be a former convenience store. There was even a faded Pepsi-Cola logo painted on the window.

"This is your computer expert?" I asked.

"He knows his shit," he said as he hopped out of the truck. "Appearances can be deceiving. Didn't anyone ever tell you that?"

"I think I might've heard that before."

There was a small bell above the door that dinged as Gord pushed it open. The thick aroma of marijuana and incense met me as we walked inside. Reggae music played in the background and it took me a moment to recognize the cover of John Denver's "Take Me Home Country Roads."

A thin man with long dreadlocks looked up from a workbench that was covered in computer components.

"Hey look who it is!" he said, "The long arm of the law!"

"How's life treating you, Chester?" Gord asked.

"Could always be worse, y'know?"

Chester stood and he and Gord exchanged a complicated hand shake, the sort that I had never been able to master, a fact that used to cause me no small embarrassment back in high school.

"Who's your friend?"

"Derek Lasker. I guess you could say he's helping me with something I'm working on."

"Good to know you," he said. He waved at me, which prevented me from looking completely incompetent in the hip handshake department.

"Thanks. You too."

"He's got a DVD that's got some kind of access code. I'm hoping you can put your larcenous skills to work and break it."

"Anything for a friend, right? 'Specially a friend with a badge!"

"Hand it over, Lasky."

I passed Chester the disc.

"What's on it?" he asked.

"Porn, probably," Gord answered, "But it could also be something relevant to a case."

Chester fed the disc into the computer. "Boys, let's hope for some bad-ass porn!"

After a moment he was faced with the same barrier that Gord had come up against earlier.

"Asking for a six-digit code," Chester said. "Do we know his birthday, anything obvious like that?"

"No," Gord said. "I'm still waiting to get his profile from

the good folks downtown. We don't even have a last name."
He turned to me. "There must've been something with his
last name on it in his office. You didn't notice anything
when you were snooping around."

"Nope, not that I saw," I answered. In actuality, I hadn't
looked for anything like that. It would have been a good
idea. There'd been some official letters in the desk that may
have had his full name on it, and I didn't even make note
of it. Very, very sloppy. But I wasn't about to let Gordo know
just how incompetent I had become.

"Can you crack it?" the big man asked.

"Anything can be done if the will's there, man. Might
take some time. You care to have a smoke while I run some
programs?"

That sounded good to me but Gord said, "How about I
leave this with you and you give me a call the second you
find anything."

"You're always in such a rush," Chester said as he lit a
huge joint and sat in a chair in front of a computer. "You
got very little faith in my technological skills, man. Six digit
code ain't nothing to the computerized mind. What's a few
million computations per second to such a beast as what I
have built here?" As he spoke he tapped away at his
keyboard and numbers began to flash too quickly to be
spotted by the human eye. The marijuana smelled great.
It'd been a long time since I had partaken and the thought
of doing so now sounded delightful. It might help me forget
that I was sleeping in the backseat of my car. I wasn't stupid;
I knew that taking drugs and/or alcohol to help forget ones
problems is a slippery slope since the drugs and/or alcohol
could become an even bigger problem than whatever issue
that caused you to seek narcotic/alcoholic abandon in the
first place. It was a moot point since Chester didn't offer me
a turn on the joint; he just sat at the computer, typing away

with the huge thing sitting at the corner of his mouth like the Marlborough Man.

"You still using that machine I built for you?" Chester asked.

"Yeah," Gord answered. "Seems to be working okay."

"Of course it be working okay! You think I do a shoddy job? I am a professional, man."

"Yeah," Gord said, "but a professional at what?"

"Building, selling and servicing computers," he said with a smile, "Nothing more."

"So you turned away from the criminal life after serving your time, huh? You still sticking to that story?"

"That's right, Gordon. Spending time in the environment of prison showed me that I do not want to go back. I be a reformed man."

"Then you'd be the first con that prison ever had that effect on."

"Oh please man, you know that's not true. Many a man's come out of prison better than when he went in." Chester paused a moment for effect, then said, "They come out a better burglar, better bank robber, better rapist, better murderer." He laughed at his joke, and the sweet-smelling smoke seemed to give his laughter a physical manifestation as it flowed from his mouth.

"And you, Chester?" Gord asked. "Did it make you a better thief?"

"No, no, no. I be following the straight and narrow road. My only concession to the dark side is the sweet ganja and you know that that is for purely spiritual purposes."

"Right. Listen, it's been nice chatting with you about the penal system and its pros and many, many cons—"

"Good one!" Chester shouted.

"—but I have better things to do with my time." He pushed me toward the door. "As for us, we are out of here.

You got my number. Call me as soon as you focus all of that spiritual energy and crack the code, okay?"

"Okay man. You are too impatient. I tell you it won't take me long but you have no faith."

"You're right," he said. "I got no faith in anything."

We walked out of the computer store and standing out on River Street at the back of the black Suburban was the scraggliest-looking prostitute I'd ever seen. The woman was obviously on some serious drugs, in need of some serious drugs, was suffering from a severe mental disease, or some combination of the three She was weaving on her feet and lifting her shirt revealing almost non-existent breasts to the passing cars.

"Twenty bucks!" she yelled at a Honda Accord. "Twenty bucks!" To a Dodge Ram.

"Get the hell out of here!" Gord yelled at her.

"It's a free country!" she snapped back, bleary-eyed and weaving. "You don't own this street!"

He pulled out his badge and held it in front of her scabby face, as if his blue combat suit and the weapons strapped all over his body wasn't enough to tell her he was a cop. "Oh no?"

She made a quick getaway, stumbling south toward Queen Street as we got into the Suburban.

"God . . ." I muttered, "Who the hell would see that woman and want to pay her to have sex?"

Gordo started the vehicle.

"Lasky, if you knew how many sick sons of bitches there were in this town, I swear to God you'd go up in a tall building and jump off. I shit you not. No sane person would want to live in this world if they knew just how awful people can be."

He put the truck into reverse.

"How can you stand it?" I asked.

"Simple," he shrugged, "I'm not sane."

As soon as backed onto River Street he slammed it into drive and as we roared a half block north to Dundas his cell rang. He picked it up as we sat at the red light. If it hadn't rung I'm sure he would have flicked on his flashing lights and blasted through the intersection, veering around oncoming vehicles and cutting off streetcars. Didn't they realize that Gordon Grossman was too important to wait for traffic lights? He listened to his phone for a moment, sighed, shut the phone without a word, put the car into reverse and floored it back to the computer store.

"He's cracked it," he said.

Chapter 25

"I told you it wouldn't take me no time at all, man!"

"Yeah, you did. You want me to call the mayor and the chief of police and organize a ticker-tape parade to honor your fine achievement or will you quit your yapping and let me see what's on the damn disc?"

Chester looked at me. "How can you work with a man that be so lacking in levity?"

"I've known him for a long time," I said, "so I guess I'm used to it."

"Watch your mouth," snapped Gord, "both of you. I'm in no mood for fun and games. There's serious heat coming down on this case and I don't want to be wasting my time, which means wasting the force's time, on a couple of comedians."

Chester held up his hands in surrender. "Okay, okay. All business it is. So my machine cracked the code and we see here that on the disc is one file, a video recording. Shall we watch it and see just what sort of kinky shit it be?"

"Just roll it already."

Chester had two monitors, both high quality flat-screens, playing the footage. At first it was very hard to make out any sort of image; there was only a sense of movement on the almost completely dark screen. The only sound on the footage was muffled, like cloth being rubbed over a microphone.

"Don't look like porn," Chester said, "at least not yet. I feel disappointed."

A light appeared in the darkness, a light that kept swinging in and out of the shot. Whoever was using the camera was not holding it steady. As the camera got closer to the light a building became visible.

"This is making me dizzy," Chester said, "Whoever shot this didn't know how to use a damn camera."

"No one's forcing you to watch," Gord said.

"What? And miss the part were the naked ladies finally appear?"

The building began to take shape. It looked like some sort of warehouse, though details were still difficult to make out in the pixilated image. It looked as if large trees surrounded it and the lack of streetlights suggested that it was somewhere secluded. We could hear the murmuring of voices, but they were too muffled to make out what was being said. As the camera moved closer to the building a door appeared with a large man standing next to it. A few words were said and he held open the door.

"He looks like security," I said.

"And the camera was pointed at his knees, you notice that?" Chester asked. "It's like this camera is hidden in a bag or something. That would explain why it keeps swing-ing around so much. Perverts like to do that sort of thing. They bring a camera into the change room of a gym and let it roll while people are undressing."

"Is that something you picked up in prison?" Gord asked.

"No, I learned that trick from TV."

We were all watching more intently as they walked inside. I say 'they' since several people were walking in front of the mysterious camera person. They walked down a hallway lit by bare bulbs that flared out the camera, and judging by the murmurs, they continued to speak to one another.

"Recognize anyone?" Gord asked me.

"I haven't seen anyone yet. A lot of shots of the back of people's legs but that's it."

There was another door ahead and the noise and light level rose dramatically once it was pushed open. Many people were in this area, which was large and open, again suggesting some sort of warehouse space. Fifty people? A hundred? It was hard to tell with the constantly swinging perspective of the camera. There was some sort of fenced area ahead. As the camera got closer I could see that it was a four-sided space made with chain-linked fence, with each side being a square about ten feet high and wide. The group of people, all quite excited judging by their volume and mannerisms, were encircling the empty fenced area.

"What's that?" Chester asked.

"Ray and Bob Junior talked a lot about cage fighting," I said. "This could be something like that."

"Someone's pirating footage of a fight?" Chester asked.

"If that's what this is," Gord said, "it's no fight sanctioned by any league. The UFC wouldn't set up shop in some warehouse in the middle of the night, would it?"

"Underground fighting is a big thing, man. Look for two minutes on the Internet and you'll see hundreds of idiots beating on each other. Look at my man Kimbo Slice," Chester said, referring to the huge fighter who made a name for himself with fights posted on YouTube, fights which took place in backyards, or parking lots. "He starts out knocking heads while a few people watch, but then his ass-whoopings get put on the Internet and viewed by millions of people and next thing you know he's fighting on TV for big money."

"If that's what we got here," Gord said, "it's illegal. I don't care how many people watch it online."

Thankfully, the bag stopped moving and the camera angle held steady. Had someone set it on a chair? It was pointed toward a man who seemed to recognize someone in the group because he walked forward with a smile on his face. The man was a short and pudgy Asian in a well-cut suit. It remained difficult to make out any details of people's faces, not only because of the camera angle, but also because there was something in front of the lens: a screen or mesh or something of that sort, which certainly lent credibility to Chester's suggestion that this was a hidden camera.

What could be seen was money.

There was a lot of it being waved around.

"Are they betting?" I asked.

"Looks like it," Chester said.

After several minutes of this, people's attention shifted to the cage, and they began to cheer. The camera shifted that direction. Someone had entered the cage from a doorway on the far side. His face was blown out by the brightness of the overhead light, but what could be seen was that he was wearing only shorts, and had some sort of glove on his left hand. He then held up his right hand in dramatic fashion, which caused a surge of volume in the roaring crowd.

In the hand was a knife, which flared the lens as it reflected the intensity of the overhead light.

The lean and extremely fit person stepped forward and as soon as he was away from the glare of the lamp, I recognized him immediately.

"That's Bob Linehan Junior," I said.

Chapter 26

"What the hell?" asked Gord. "Don't tell me they have some sort of underground knife fighting operation! The crazy sons of bitches. And you said this is a high school kid?"

"Yeah. Goes to Winston Churchill Collegiate."

"Christ . . ."

"Starting to look like this porn movie be more like a snuff movie, y'know?" Chester said. "Which ain't my cup of tea, but I hear there's big money in it."

People moved in between the camera and Bob Junior so whoever was operating the camera pushed closer to the cage and put the bag on the ground . The camera had a skewed view of the ring and Bob Junior was moving in and out of the shot as he danced in preparation for what was to come. There was, however, a perfect view of the entrance to the cage.

"Holy shit," I said when I saw what was happening at that entrance. There were two gates leading into the cage, forming a pen area where you were through one door but not the second. It wasn't another fighter that was in that area, at least not a human one. It was a dog, a big one. We could see it thrashing in there with ferocious anger.

"Are they poking it with sticks?" Chester asked.

"Looks that way." Judging by the deep timbre of Gord's voice, he would have liked to use a stick on the men who were poking the dog through the cage. "They're whipping it into a frenzy, or more like poking it."

All the while, Bob Junior stood motionless, his knife at his side, watching them abuse the dog. We could only see part of the right side of his body since the camera was focused on the poor animal.

"What kind of dog is that?" Chester asked. "Pit bull?"

"Rottweiler," Gord said. He was really upset, at least as upset as the big man could get. His voice seemed close to breaking. Did that mean he had a soft spot for animals? Wow. Maybe Gordo was human after all. "Damn good dogs. Unless they are abused and then . . ." He didn't need to finish. We'd all read stories in the papers about the dogs attacking people, sometimes even killing them.

The Rottweiler was snapping, trying to get at the people who were attacking it, and then suddenly the door between it and Bob Junior swung open.

"Oh Jesus . . ." Chester whispered as the dog rushed toward Bob Junior, a big black rocket, so full of rage that foam was frothing from its mouth. The camera angle did not allow us to see exactly what happened next, but it was less than thirty seconds later that we saw something that made us all jump and then wince. The lifeless body of the dog fell into shot, its dead eyes staring straight into the lens. The dog was twitching and we could see blood spurting several feet into the air from a horrid wound on its neck. The doors to the cage opened and people rushed inside and lifted Bob into the air like he had just won the lightweight belt. I recognized two of the faces.

"Two of them go to school with Bob. I saw them leave with him the other day." I had taken pictures of them as they had walked from the school to the Civic.

"The little bastard . . ." Gord growled. "I'll kill him . . ."

Then something happened to the camera—it was bumped on purpose or accidentally, but it rolled on its side and all we could see were people's feet moving through the frame.

"Can I play this on any DVD player now?" Gord asked.

Chester stopped the DVD and tapped a few keys. "Ok, there you go. I locked in the code so it will play on any player as long as it isn't too old."

We were all shaken by what we had just witnessed. I felt numb. "What kind of people would—"

"People that are in for a whole goddamned world of trouble," Gord snapped, his eyes flaring with anger. "Give me the disc."

Chester popped it out of his computer, put it back into the case and handed it to him quickly. Gord's tone warned one not to delay lest his anger be turned upon them.

"How many of these discs did you find in his drawer?"

"At least a dozen."

"The son of a bitch. I can't wait to get my hands on him. Thanks, Chester."

"Okay, no prob." He brought his hands up and rubbed his eyes, as if wanted to rid them of the grotesque image of the butchered Rottweiler.

"Let's go," said Gord, and I followed him out of the store.

The scraggly prostitute was at the back of the truck again, attempting to sell her wares. Gord ran at her. Before she could get away, he grabbed her by the shoulders and, lifting her up like she was weightless, screamed into her face loud enough to make me jump. "I TOLD YOU TO GET THE HELL OUT OF HERE! NOW DISAPPEAR BEFORE I BREAK YOUR MISERABLE BODY IN HALF!"

She stumbled backward when he let her go but somehow retained her footing. With fear on her face, she ran as fast as an Olympic sprinter away from the big man.

I said nothing about the shocking scene as I got into the vehicle. It had been an all together unpleasant morning.

"I am going to kill that kid ten times over," said Gord. "How can we find him?"

Considering the state he was in, I wondered for a moment whether I wanted to sic Gordon Grossman on Bob Junior, but considering the ferocity of his glare, refusing him was clearly not an option.

"I have a tracer in his Civic," I said, "Take me back to my car and we can find him."

Chapter 27

It was a white-knuckle ride eastward.

We roared across the city, and I was glad that we were encased in such a tank of a vehicle since it afforded some manner of protection should we crash into one of the many vehicles or pedestrians we swerved around during the frightful journey. More than one person was forced to leap out of our way as we barreled through flashing pedestrian crosswalks. No music was playing during this trip since there was no room in the vehicle for melody or rhythm, not with Gord's seething anger taking up so much space. His eyes were on the road and I could see his jaw twitching, like he was imagining taking a bite out of someone's throat.

"Tell me everything you know about this Bob Linehan Junior," he said.

"Okay . . . where to start. He's seventeen, goes to Winston Churchill Collegiate, his dad said he wasn't an A student and I got the sense that he wasn't much of a student at all, he drives a customized Honda Civic that must have cost a fortune, his parents don't like that he hangs out with some black kids who they think are gangbangers, he has a closet full of knives which his parents know about and don't think is strange, he—"

"Goddamned parents! Why can't there be one set of them that don't screw up their kids?"

"I'm sure there must be some out there that don't—"

"What else?"

"Okay, his dad, Bob Senior, thought that his kid murdered the neighbor's cat and left it headless in his backyard, which is why he called me in the first place. He and his kid seem to fight a lot, but if I thought my kid was decapitating the neighbor's pet I guess I would be pretty—"

"Stick to facts, Lasky. I don't care about how you would raise your own hypothetical offspring."

"Okay, just the facts." Chester wasn't kidding when he said dealing with Gordon was a trying experience. "Bob Junior teaches a course at Ray's dojo, a course in knife fighting, he seems to idolize Ray and keeps talking about what a great fighter he is, that he could be a UFC middleweight champ. We both know that Bob Junior does some cage fighting of his own and if he's making money knife fighting maybe that's how he can afford such an expensive car."

"Do you think he put the cat head in front of the school?"

"I don't know one hundred percent, but if I was a betting man, which I'm not because I'm broke, I would lay down some money on it, yeah. If you're going to ask me if I have any idea whose tongue might be inside the cat's mouth, I don't. Bob Senior seems pretty sure that the cat head belonged to his neighbor's cat and that it's the missing piece of the animal he found in the backyard, and that he buried there shortly after finding it."

Gord pulled his mobile from a pocket on his chest and hit a speed dial number. "Jen, it's Grossman." Pause. "Yeah it's a bad one and getting even worse. I want you to look into a Robert Linehan Senior, people call him Bob." He spelled the name and had me read out his address that I scrambled to find in my small notebook. "Send it to my laptop. Thanks, doll." To me he said, "Tell me more."

"As soon as the story about the cat head was on the news, Bob Senior fired me and when you boys called him to check up on me he denied ever hiring me in the first place, said he never hired a P.I. in his life."

"Yeah, yeah, I know."

"But you have my phone! You must have checked—"

"Yeah, yeah. You got numbers to and from him in your mobile which may mean you are telling the truth."

"May mean? Are you saying there is still some question?"

"There's other reasons you could be exchanging calls with the guy. It doesn't you're working for him. Lasky, you know damn well that there are men in the force who would love to make you for this caper. They think you got that lone nut feel about you and as much as I try to say you aren't as crazy as you seem, the more they say that I'm just a guy who kicks in doors and busts heads so what do I know about judging people?" He laid on the horn and swerved around a fat man on a Harley Davidson and startled the rider so much that he wobbled and nearly tipped the big bike. Gordo chuckled. "Are they right, Lasky? Are you a lone nut?"

"No!"

"Okay, so maybe you've got some buddies somewhere and you're not a lone nut. Are you a nut of any variety?"

"Come on, Gordo, I'm just a guy trying to make a living. I'm no more crazy than you.'

"But I'm completely nuts, Lasky. Haven't you known me long enough to figure that out?"

I couldn't argue with that point. "But surely the video shows that Bob Junior is——"

"I know what it shows," he snapped. "I was right there watching it with you, remember? That's why we're going to find the little bastard and I'm going to ask him some questions and you know what? I hope the punk pulls a knife on me. I would make him suffer, Lasky. I would kill him slow and call it self-defense, a righteous kill."

Gordon was very scary when he started talking about how badly he wanted to kill people. I didn't feel very good about leading Gordo to Bob Junior if he was intent on killing him the moment he felt he could do so without facing legal repercussions.

I decided to do my best to be present when he met with Bob Junior to ensure that they didn't kill each other. It wasn't just that I didn't want any more killing, I didn't really care if the dog-and-cat-killing kid lived or died, but I wanted him alive long enough to admit that he did indeed kill Mittens and put her head on a stick in front of the school, and that I cracked the case and deserved the reward money.

After that fat pile of bills was in my hands, Gordo could kill him slow, fast, or any way he wanted and I couldn't care less.

Chapter 28

"He's not far," I said, looking down at my tracer while standing next to my Corolla.

"We'll leave your car here," Gord said. "Come on."

I didn't mind riding with him since the moment I ran out of gas my car would no longer be my mobile home, as I hadn't the money to refuel. Some change in my pocket and dreams of a $10,000 payday was all I had. I could sell the car for a few hundred, maybe even a grand, and another few hundred for my various surveillance gear, but how long would that money last me? And that would surely mark the end of the all-but-dead Lasker Investigations. Who would hire a P.I. who needed to take public transit?

After thinking of what little of value I owned, I grabbed my bag of equipment from the trunk, wanting to keep it close, and climbed into the front seat of the Suburban. Gord was looking at something on the laptop mounted between the seats.

"You said Bob Linehan Senior was a forklift operator?"

"That's what he told me. He said he got his license when he was seventeen and has been working ever since."

"You really need to get your bullshit sensors recalibrated, Lasky. He owns a company called DMC Industries. They make hydraulic industrial equipment and do pretty well at it. Just got a big contract with Bombardier to make a piece of the landing gear on some new model of plane."

"Oh." I felt like an idiot. "That makes sense because when I first met him, he didn't seem like a forklift operator," I said in an attempt to save some face. Once I thought back on it, he never did actually say that he was currently a forklift operator, just that he once was. I'd never even thought to ask him what he did for a living, and when he fired me in the parking lot of DMC he was wearing a button-down shirt, which certainly was incongruous with a warehouse worker. More evidence of my sloppiness. If I ever managed to get the $10,000, perhaps I would have to take some P.I. courses to re-learn how to do my job. More and more, the evidence seemed to be telling me that my past year of despair had seriously eroded my investigatory abilities.

Gord started the vehicle and I told him to turn left. Though my skills had been put into question, my technology was working for me and I followed my tracer easily.

"I know this building," I said as we pulled into the parking lot. "This is where Bob Junior dropped off two of his friends."

We drove around to the back and there was the orange Civic parked behind a barrier of huge overflowing trash bins being attacked by seagulls, squirrels, and all other manner of vermin. The car wouldn't be spotted by anyone not looking for it since the bins hid it from view.

"Almost looks like someone wanted to hide it."

"If you were parking a cherry ride in this place you'd make sure it was hidden too. Do you have the names of his friends?"

"No, just a picture."

Gord sighed. "You excel at giving me partial information, you know that?"

"I led you right to the car, didn't I?"

"But there must be twenty storeys in this building. Do you think we should go knock on each door to see if they have a visitor named Bob Junior?"

"I can give you the photo of them. Surely someone at the school could identify the guys. If you asked some teachers they might even know their names. Maybe even the superintendent of the building, if this dump has such a person."

"Or your old friend Bob Senior might."

"Maybe, but I don't think he's too familiar with Bob Junior's friends."

"I'm sure you'll understand if I don't trust your judgment right now, especially in regards to the supposed forklift driver."

Though I was trying to keep it in check, I was beginning to lose my temper. "I'm trying to help you with this, Gordon, so I don't know why you feel the need to continually berate me when I'm—"

"Helping me? Is that what you're doing? Oh that's funny because I thought you were chasing the reward. Huh? Aren't you? Aren't you thrilled that I'm letting you ride with me so that you can maybe find out who whacked the cat and then you can be the Humane Society's Man of the Year?"

"I could be out there on my own working this case and not share any information with you and—"

"And if it wasn't for me you would still be locked up and Mike would probably be beating you with a phone book trying to get you to confess to kitty murder!"

"So you want me to thank you for being the hero, is that it? Gord Grossman, always the hero!"

"That's right, Lasky, I always am, and I'm getting damned tired of your sorry-assed moaning! I should take you back to 43 Division and let them lock you up again! You didn't like that too much did you? You sure were happy to see me, weren't you? You could have kissed me when I said I was cutting you lose!"

"But without me you wouldn't have the DVD, you wouldn't know what Bob Junior was up to, and you wouldn't even know he existed!"

"So you're the hero? Is that it?"

"Look, all I'm saying is that I'm not a chump who deserves to be put down all the time by a guy he's trying to work with, all right?"

My mobile rang, which gave me a perfect opportunity to step out of the parked vehicle and cool down. Sure I was angry with Gordon, but I didn't want to lose him as an ally since, as he pointed out, there were those on the force who would love to lock me up in an interrogation room for a day or two and see what they could shake out of me.

I looked at my phone and was surprised to see who was calling.

"Well, well, well," I began, "if it isn't Bob Linehan Senior."

"Hi Derek. I know you must be angry with me. The police told me that they had you in custody—"

"Which wouldn't have happened if I hadn't taken your case!"

"I know that, and I'm sorry. Honestly. The thing is, Derek, I need your help."

I had to laugh. "Are you kidding? You want me to help you after you lied to the police? They wanted to arrest me, Bob. One truthful word from you and I would have been released, but instead I spent hours being questioned by—"

"I understand you're angry. You have every right. I deserve your anger. I know I have behaved very badly but this isn't about you and me, it's about my son. I need your help because Bob Junior didn't come home last night and me and my wife are worried."

"He's seventeen." I looked up at the tall brown ugly building. "He's probably at a friend's place drinking beer and playing videogames."

"I don't think so. In spite of everything I've said to you about him, he's still a kid in a lot of ways. He's never stayed out without calling before. He'd never do that to his mother.

Please, I'm begging you. I don't know who else to call. Let me hire you back."

Those words cut through my anger. "I'll meet with you but not for a measly $175 per day. I'm going to expect a sizable increase."

"That's fine and more than fair."

"And a week's pay in advance."

"Fine, fine. Just come over to the house as soon as you can. My wife is frantic."

I told him I'd be there soon and I disconnected.

Chapter 29

I pulled up outside of the Linehan residence thirty minutes later. When I told Gordon about the phone call, he wanted to come with me. I managed to convince him that it would be better if I went alone since the Linehans may say more to a private citizen that they would to a cop. Bob Senior was worried that his son was a cat-killer and was trying to protect him from the law, so why would he be forthright with the police? So went my argument. Gord went for it on the condition that I call him and tell him everything that happened. Meanwhile he would take the photos he uploaded from my digital camera and find the apartment number of Bob Junior's friends.

"We both know he's probably up there with them right now," I'd said to Gord, "and as soon as you find him his parents can stop worrying. But for now, talking to his parents and nosing around his house might help us build a case against the kid, right?"

Gord reluctantly agreed and, after calling in a couple squad cars to keep an eye on the apartment building in case Bob Junior exited, he drove me to my Corolla.

The truth was that I wanted to go see Bob Senior alone so that I could get the money he promised me. Now believe it or not, I do have some ethics and I don't make a habit of fleecing clients (except for the big insurance companies who had very deep pockets). But I felt Bob Senior owed me some compensation for what I'd gone through at 43 Division and I was going to see that I was paid. I asked for the week in advance since at that point I assumed Gord would call me within the hour to tell me that they had Bob Junior in custody, perhaps even while I was with his parents, and then I could walk smugly away from the

Linehans with a bit of money in my pocket (sorry, Bob Senior, no refunds, a deal is a deal) while I waited for the five-figure payday I hoped would come.

As I walked toward the house I saw that there was a woman working in the garden in the house next door. She caught my eye because her white shirt with three buttons undone allowed for quite a wonderful view of her bosom. Her long blonde hair shone in the bright late morning sun. She may have been a year or two older than me, but she was drop-dead gorgeous and had my heart rate increasing before I was halfway across the street. This must have been Mitten's owner. I searched my memory for her name, which Bob Senior had mentioned at our first meeting. Then she looked up at me with emerald green eyes that were so stunning they nearly made me mute.

"Mrs. Peterson?"

She straightened up and put a hand on her hip. "It's Ms. Peterson, thank you very much." She fixed me with a smile and I liked her all the more for her spunkiness.

I had to remind myself that I wasn't there to flirt with this beautiful woman—that there was something I wanted to speak to her about. "Bob mentioned that your cat has gone missing."

Her eyes turned tender. "He told you about that?"

"Yes. He must really like that cat."

"That Bob . . ." Her smile was making my head swim. "He's very considerate. He loves to come visit Mittens and is always stopping by."

Looking at Ms. Peterson I was beginning to understand why. I have no love for cats but if it meant spending some time with this beauty I would fake it. I wondered if Bob Senior was faking it too.

"He mentioned that he feeds it when you and your husband are traveling."

"He did? No, you must be mistaken. My husband travels so much with his business that when he has time off all he wants to do is sit in the backyard and look out over the lake. I don't remember the last time I had a getaway."

"I see." Why had Bob Senior lied to me about that? "Well enjoy your gardening. I hope your cat comes back."

"Thank you."

I managed to turn and walk to the Linehan home without falling over after speaking with the mind-swimmingly stunning Ms. Peterson and I knocked on the door. I turned to take one last look at the gorgeous gardener and jumped when the door was pulled open almost instantly.

"Derek," Bob said, shaking my hand with vigor. "Thank you so much for coming. I sincerely apologize for treating you so poorly. I mean it."

He looked very distraught and if I wasn't so desperate I would have felt guilty for the money I was going to take from him. The fact that I felt even a twinge of guilt relieved me, as it reminded me that I was not completely void of compassion.

"That's okay, Bob. I understand your motivations. You wanted to protect your son."

"That's right," he said as he led me into his lovely and well-appointed home, "and now we need to find him."

His wife sat on a chair in the living room and she looked twice as upset as her husband. She was an overweight woman, who looked like she had been crying for hours. Under different circumstances, I imagine Mrs. Linehan would have been quite pretty, but not with a red tear-stained face and uncombed mass of curly black hair.

"Derek Lasker, this is my wife Dorothy."

"Pleased to meet you," I said as I moved forward to shake her hand. She only nodded in reply and looked as if she was about to break into tears again.

"Derek is going to help us find Bob Junior, Dotty. You'll see."

"I hope so. It's not like him to stay out, Mr. Lasker." I asked her to call me Derek. "He's never done it before. Sure he's stayed at friends' places before but he always calls. That's why we bought him the cell phone."

"And he's not answering?" I asked.

"No," Bob replied. "I've been trying since I woke up this morning and saw that he wasn't home. His bedroom door was open and his bed hadn't been slept in."

"Oh Bob," she wailed, 'I just know something terrible has happened to him!" Great sobs poured from her and Bob sat next to her and held her as she cried into his chest. "A mother knows! A mother knows!"

"Have you tried calling his friends? I know you mentioned that he hung out with a couple of . . . hip hop boys from his high school. Would you have their names or numbers?" I could pass them on to Gord and show him that I wasn't a complete chump.

"I don't know their numbers," Bob replied. "They don't even call each other by names . . . just nicknames. They called Bob Junior 'B' like they're too damned lazy to use his full name."

"Ohhhh . . . where is my Bobby?"

"He'll be okay, Dotty"

"Stop saying that!" she cried, her tone harsh and ragged, "A mother knows . . . just like a wife knows, Bob!"

"We brought in Derek to help us, dear. He'll find Bob Junior, you'll see."

"Have you reported his disappearance to the police?"

This made Dotty wail again.

"We . . . we don't want to do that. Not yet, at least," he said. "We thought we'd give you some time to find him.

Besides, wouldn't they just tell us to wait twenty-four hours?"

"Maybe. I'm not sure."

"So how are you going to handle it?" he asked. "Where will you start?"

"I'll track down his friends and talk to them—see if someone knows where he is. Does he have a girlfriend?"

"No," he answered. "At least not that I know of."

"That's because he never talks to you!" Dotty yelled. "He is seeing a girl named Kathy Cramer. She goes to school with him."

Bob looked at his wife with surprise. "What? How long has this been going on?"

"A few months," she said. It appeared as if she enjoyed having this secret from her husband. "I even had a coffee with her and Bob one evening. She's a very sweet girl. Very pretty."

I could see Bob was angry and trying to bite back harsh words.

"I'll find her number and talk to her. Maybe he stayed out with her and didn't call because he didn't want to get into trouble."

"Oh, he's in trouble all right," Bob Senior said, "putting me and his mother through this. I had to leave the office!"

"You will not give him the slightest bit of trouble!" Dotty yelled. "If you say one cross word to him, I swear to God that it will be the last word you utter in this house!"

This domestic scene was making me extremely uncomfortable so I said, "Do you mind if I look around his room?"

"Why?" Bob asked.

"I might see something that'll give me an indication of where he might be."

"Okay, then. I don't see why not," he answered. "It's in the basement, to the right of the stairs."

"And I'm going to need to talk to you soon, Bob, about the details we talked about on the phone."

"Okay. I have what you need."

Good, I thought.

I felt bad for poor Dotty and was hoping that Gord would call and relieve her worries, but not before her husband gave me my money. Granted, she'd have a new set of worries once she found out her son was arrested, but at least she'd know where he was, which would amount to some consolation.

I was hoping that if Gord had tracked down Bob Junior that the boy survived his encounter with the big man and that Gord hadn't tossed the kid off of the balcony and then told investigators that the kid jumped after confessing his deep shame at killing Mittens and that he, Gordon Grossman, felt terrible that he'd been unable to reach the boy in time to save him from the twenty-storey fall.

Bob Junior's bedroom was spotless, clean with military precision, unlike the bedrooms of most seventeen year old boys who had clothes, magazines, dirty dishes and all manner of things scattered on the floor. The bed was made perfectly and every item on the desk and dresser was lined up with geometric precision. There were posters of fighters on the walls, but not being a fan I didn't recognize any of the names. There were also posters of hip-hop musicians whom I also didn't know. At least the posters made the kid seem normal, unlike the spotlessness of the room. Maybe the Linehan's had a maid, a very good and thorough maid.

To my right was the famous knife-filled closet that Bob Senior had told me about. I walked to it and opened the doors.

Chapter 30

The closet was divided into two halves and even that simple fact seemed ripe with psychological significance.

On the right were clothes hung with the same neatness as the rest of the room and beneath those hangers was a shelf that held shoes, mostly sneakers of various brands and colors all lined up with the laces carefully tucked into the body of the shoe. These were peaceful innocuous items used in everyday life.

The left side, (which, I suddenly recalled, was the side associated with both the devil and creativity) was filled with weapons of death. These were not the knives that I had been expecting, but all manner of bladed weapons from several nations and eras whose sole purpose was to chop the human form into two or more pieces.

I didn't know the names of most of the weapons, but I recognized the short samurai sword—I even recalled from some movie that it was called a *tanto*. And I recognized the odd-looking knife called a *gurkha*. There were big bowie knives, fat short swords, serrated knives, long thin daggers, double-edged knives that looked like shrunken versions of medieval swords, and many other strange and deadly-looking weapons. If I was hoping to find a weapon crusted with dry blood that would lock up this case, I was to be disappointed. They were all clean, shiny, and sharp.

I didn't know the ins and outs of what constituted a legal or illegal bladed weapon, but I suspected that several of the blades mounted carefully, even reverently, on the left half of the closet were illegal. I'd brought my bag down with me and snapped pictures of the blades, finishing up when I heard footsteps coming down the stairs. I dropped the camera back into the bag just as Bob Senior entered the room.

"Find anything?" he asked sharply.

"Excuse me?"

"Find anything useful? Anything that will help you find my son or are you just snooping?"

"You mentioned that he had knives in his closet and I thought I'd take a look."

"Do you really think that's going to help you find him?" Was it his concern for his missing son that was causing him to be so aggressive?

"An investigator can never know what will prove to be useful and needs to keep an open and curious mind."

That seemed to satisfy him. He sighed. "I'm sorry, Derek. I shouldn't be angry with you."

"No, I should be angry with you."

"Yeah, but now I need you to focus on finding my son." He handed me a piece of paper with a name and phone number. "That's the girl my wife was talking about."

"That's a good place to start." He really did seem upset about the whole situation and I guess I had difficulty understanding since I don't have kids. As for me, I remembered what I was like at seventeen and staying out all night was not an uncommon occurrence, especially once I was fortunate enough to become sexually active, and upon my return the next day, my parents yelled at me but weren't sitting on the couch with tears running down their faces and calling a down-on-his-luck private investigator to find me. Maybe things are different today. Everyone is concerned about serial killers, perverts, and terrorists hiding in every shadow.

"I'm ready to get started if you could give me the fee we discussed."

"Right, right," he said. "How much would a week come to?"

I was going to ask for more, but felt guilty so I said, "Let's just start at $500 and I'll let you know when that runs out."

He pulled out a wallet and pulled out five hundreds. I looked at the brown bills. I don't know if I had ever seen a hundred dollar bill before and judging by the thick wad that remained in his wallet I kicked myself for not asking for the grand instead. Oh well. I assumed that I would be calling them within the hour to say that crazy Gordo had their son in his clutches so the $500 would seem like a better deal then.

"Okay, I'll get started. I'll keep you posted on my progress."

I walked past him and moved toward the stairs with him behind me then I turned and asked him, "A funny thing . . . I was talking to your neighbor, Ms. Peterson, and she said that she can't remember the last time she went on vacation."

He stared at me with a mystified expression. "So?"

"Well . . . it's just that you told me that you used to watch Mittens for free when Ms. Peterson and her husband were away, yet she said that wasn't the case."

"I never said that. I said I went over there to visit and I liked the cat but it was to see Mason, not Mittens."

"Mason?"

"Mason Peterson. He's a top honcho at Bombardier and a good friend. Shame he has to travel so much, but if it wasn't for him working so hard his company wouldn't be doing so well."

"And wouldn't be able to give DMC a big contract," I added.

The surprise struck him and he reacted as if I'd right then slapped him across the face. "You know about that?"

"We, at Lasker Investigations, are very thorough."

"I can see that. It hasn't even been announced to the press yet and is still not carved in stone. How did you hear about it?"

"I'm not at liberty to say."

He reached out and took hold of my arm just above the elbow, tight enough that it hurt, to get my attention and to keep me from going up the stairs. "But there are secrecy clauses written all over this contract so I don't see how you could have found out about it."

I pulled my arm away, fighting the temptation to push the smaller man. "Listen, Bob, I have some powerful friends who have access. That's why you hired me in the first place, isn't it? Because I can uncover things that Joe Citizen can't?"

I didn't like the sharp and suspicious look he was giving me, (as if he was contemplating sticking one of Bob Junior's knives into my belly) and I was beginning to realize that there was more to this Bob Linehan Senior that I had original thought. He had secrets of his own and his son wasn't the only one with a dark side.

"Okay," he said, the anger not leaving his eyes. "Just find my boy."

I went up the stairs and glanced into the living room and saw that Dotty was no longer there. Then I made good my escape from the oddness of the Linehan home. There were strange things going on in that household; my rusty skills were screaming at me about that.

I was sorry to see Ms. Peterson was no longer in her yard or I'm sure I would have let professionalism be damned and not even have bothered to go through the motions of looking for Bob Junior and flirted with her instead.

Chapter 31

I called Gord as I pulled away.

I was driving back toward Kingston Road, where I planned to buy some lunch with my newly acquired money once I'd found some place to break the big bills. I was also going to buy some cigarettes since I was feeling a low-grade headache after going without for the past day.

"I saw the closet full of knives."

"And?"

"I took pictures. I bet there's a lot of illegal blades in there."

"Did you see anything that matched the blade we saw in the video?"

"Hard to say. There were a few that looked like it. There were thirty or forty in there."

"What else? The parents tell you anything?"

"Nothing solid, but I'm getting more suspicious about Bob Senior."

"What is it with you and the forklift driver?"

I told him about the lie he had told me about cat sitting for Ms. Peterson and his feeble excuse.

"Maybe it's like he said and you just heard him wrong."

"I didn't."

"Maybe he was trying to keep the Bombardier deal quiet."

I didn't want to listen to Gord put down my hunches. It was bad enough that I was losing faith in myself and I didn't need others to make me feel even worse so I changed the subject. "Did you find the apartment number?"

"Yeah. I'm just on my way back to the building right now."

"How about I meet you there so that I can—"

"I don't need your help on this, Lasky. I can kick in a

door all by myself. Keep in touch." And he disconnected.

What to do?

Should I drive over to the apartment building to keep my promise to be there when he nabbed Bob Junior, or continue to go through the motions and call Kathy Cramer and pretend to look for a boy who is about to be found all to earn my 500 bucks?

I decided that Bob Junior was on his own and I would call Kathy, but first, coffee and cigarettes.

Considering that the police already had photos of me from the day I was watching Bob Junior and his friends, I was concerned about the school's surveillance cameras snapping another photo of me, so I asked Kathy Cramer to meet me down the block. I didn't need the cops to become even more suspicious. I'd called Kathy and she answered her mobile on the first ring and agreed to meet me during her lunch break.

I was outside of my car leaning against the hood reading a red hardcover copy of Macbeth that I'd found in the trunk of my car. The trunk was full of all sorts of bric-a-brac that I hadn't the heart to part with. This Bob Junior affair had me wanting to find the passage about the dagger that, like so much of Shakespeare, I only half remembered, and I found Macbeth's famous soliloquy in Act II, Scene i:

Is this a dagger, which I see before me?
The handle toward my hand? Come, let me clutch thee.
I have thee not, and yet I see thee still.
Art thou not, fatal vision, sensible
To feeling, as to sight? or art thou but
A dagger of the mind, a false creation,
Proceeding from the heat-oppressed brain?

I looked up marveling at the beauty and insight of Shakespeare's words and two girls were suddenly before me like Macbeth's ghostly dagger.

"You Derek Lasker?" one of them asked. They were both tough-looking kids.

"That's right. And you're Kathy Cramer?"

"Yeah."

"Nice car," her friend said before breaking into laughter. Kathy joined her.

I bit back a cutting retort since these were teenagers. Let them make fun of the old Corolla if they wanted to. The car could take it and my pride was too battered to care.

"Have you seen or heard from Bob Linehan Junior since yesterday?" I asked.

They both broke out into a new round of laughter.

"What's so funny?"

"He never said he was a junior!" said Kathy's friend.

"Junior!" Kathy laughed. "Wait 'til we tell everyone! Junior! Junior!"

Then her friend joined her: "Junior! Junior! Junior! Junior!"

"So," I yelled to be heard over their chanting, "have you seen him?"

"Like, why is this guy even asking you these questions?" asked the friend. "He a cop or something?"

"Because," she said impatiently, "his parents think he's, like, missing or something."

"And is he?" I asked.

"How should I know?"

"Has he been at school today?"

"I haven't seen him."

"Would you usually see him?"

"Yeah!" said her friend. "They be, like, getting busy in his ride every day at lunchtime!"

"Shut up!"

"You know it be true, K!"

"At least I got a man that, like, wants to be with me and stuff."

"Ohhhhh! You know there be plenty of boys crawling around after all this," she said, indicating her body, which looked plump and child-like to me. Talking to them was getting very tedious. How did high school teachers keep from going insane? Or were they all insane and hid it relatively well?

"So you haven't seen him?" I asked.

"No," Kathy answered.

"And you haven't talked to him on the phone?"

"No."

"And you have no idea where he might be?"

"I ain't, like, seen or talked to him since, like, yesterday."

"You ain't?" I asked, not doing a good job of hiding my sarcastic tone. "Did he ever mention a man named Ray, or what he did at the martial arts gym?"

"No," Kathy answered. "I never knew he was into all that."

"You going to tell us that, like, Junior on the down low with this Ray?"

"Shut up!" Kathy yelled.

"I'm only asking!"

Enough is enough. My patience was about to snap. "Like, thanks girls," I said.

I got into my car but not before I heard Kathy's friend say, "Like, what a loser!"

I started the car and pulled away.

I lit a cigarette to help calm my foul mood.

Again I was mystified that any sane adult would ever wish to return to their teens. It's a horrible age and if you don't remember it that way you're fooling yourself.

Depressing to think that these, like, girls and Bob Junior and his buddies were our nation's future.

Back in 1987, if a man twenty years older than me had observed my infantile jock behavior, certainly he too would have bemoaned the future of the species. Looking at the wreck I'd become, filching 500 bucks off of a desperate parent, living in a car, losing his patience during a two-minute talk with teenagers, having few prospects other than chasing a $10,000 dream, it appeared that the hypothetical man had been proven right. I hoped for their own sakes that Kathy and her smart-mouthed friend would do a better job with their lives than I had with mine.

Chapter 32

I drove to the apartment building since Gord wasn't answering his phone. When I got there I saw three cruisers in the parking lot restricting access to the building, as well as two black police Suburbans. I parked my car and walked toward the first cop, who had a familiar face.

"Officer Papineau!" I called out with a smile. "How are you?"

"Not you again . . ."

"Is that any way to treat a fellow protector of the public good?"

Her face scrunched up into a look of disbelief. "Is that what you believe yourself to be?"

"Sure. A private investigator serves a valuable role in a free society."

"If you say so. Besides, word is you don't even have a license."

"I do, it just expired."

"Uh huh."

"It was just a simple bookkeeping error."

"Right."

"Did Grossman find Bob Junior?"

"What business would that be of yours?"

"I led him to this building this morning. We're working together on this thing."

She looked unconvinced. "Right. Like I told you the other day at the school, you need to step away. Get back in your car and go. Let the real police take care of this."

I ignored her barbed words. "I've been trying to call Grossman but he isn't answering his mobile. How about you call him on your radio. I'm sure he'd want me to come up."

"You telling me what to do?"

"No." This was almost as frustrating as talking to the teenagers. "But if you just contact him and let him know I'm here, I'm sure he'd want to know about it. I know things about the kid that might help."

"What kid?"

"Bob Linehan Junior."

She looked at me like I was a piece of dog doo that was fouling the bottom of her black police boot (it was a look she was very good at, judging by the fact that it rarely left her face when she was dealing with me). But then she took a few steps back to the other side of the car and began speaking into the handset that was mounted near her right shoulder. She turned back to me.

"He's on the 12th floor."

"Thank you, Officer Papineau. You know something?" I asked as I walked past her. "I'm a nice guy once you get to know me."

"I'll have to take your word for it."

I walked into the building and was not pleased to see an out of service sign taped to the sole elevator. Someone had written a harsh criticism of the building's owners (along with a crude drawing) on the sign.

Great.

Twelve flights of stairs.

Good thing I'd stopped at Tim Horton's and had a hearty chili lunch before my meeting with Kathy; I was going to need the energy.

I was short of breath by the time I made it up to the 12th floor. The trip had not been pleasant. I am not a religious man, but if there is a hell and eternal torture therein, I imagine spending endless centuries climbing the stairwells in that building would be worse than anything Dante had ever come up with.

Animal and human excrement, rotting food, cigarette

butts, the occasional crack pipe, beer and liquor bottles (both broken and unbroken), urine, empty pop bottles, crushed Tim Horton's cups, plastic grocery bags, assorted McDonalds waste, empty aerosol paint cans, used condoms, old newspapers, empty potato chip bags, soiled disposable diapers, cockroaches, mice (or were they rats?), silverfish, houseflies, fruit flies, discarded shoes and clothing, and unidentifiable sticky substances accompanied each step.

Part of my being so short of breath was caused by the twelve-storey climb (which I did in record time), but it was also due to the fact that I took as few breaths as possible during my climb up the foul stairwell. By comparison, the air in the hallway smelled as sweet as a country field in springtime.

The cops were congregating at the far end and I made my way toward them. There was a mixture of regular uniformed cops and a couple of Special Task Force men as well. I guess Gord wanted to make sure his department got in on the fun.

One of the uniforms turned to me as I got close. "You Lasker?"

I said I was.

"Go on in."

Wow. That was more like it!

"Thanks," I said to him.

As I entered the apartment, which was much nicer than the stairwells suggested, I saw Gord pacing in front of the two teens that I'd seen Bob Junior drop off the other day. A video game was paused on the large television behind Gord and a controller was on the table in front of each teen. One had elaborate cornrows that truly were a work of art and the other had a well-maintained afro complete with hair pick stuck into it. They had their hands behind their backs and I assume they had been cuffed. I saw no sign of Bob Junior.

"You expect me to buy that?" Gord asked them.

"I told you!" said the teen with the afro. "We don't know how the car got there! We didn't even know it be out there! We ain't seen Bob since yesterday afternoon."

"You didn't take part in some knife-fighting last night? Some cage fighting?"

I could see Gord's knowledge of that startled the kids, but they tried to hide it.

"I don't know what you're talking about."

"We got you on tape, sunshine. Coming into the cage and lifting up Junior after he slaughtered a Rottweiler. You know killing animals is a crime, don't you? So is being involved in underground fighting. So is gambling on those fights. We got you involved in all of this."

"Damn . . ." afro muttered.

The cornrow kid looked the tougher of the two and just stared at Gordon with steely determination, as if he wouldn't tell him the time of day even if Gord shoved bamboo under his fingernails. And I wouldn't be surprised if Gord had done that and worse during his career.

Gord continued, "You're under eighteen but close enough that I could get them to charge you as adults which would mean a few years in the Pen. How's that for a good way to start adulthood, huh? It's up to you, college or prison."

"We don't know nothing!" cornrow yelled.

"I know you were at that fight."

"What fight?" cornrow asked.

"Yeah, fine," afro admitted. "We was there."

"Shut up, man!"

"I ain't going to miss college for this!" said afro. "I already got accepted to film school!"

"I want to hear all about those fights, everything you know," Gord said, "but first, where's Bob Linehan?"

Afro looked up at Gord with a look that appeared sincere. "We ain't seen him since yesterday afternoon and that's the honest truth."

"But he had a knife-fighting class last night," Gord said.

"We don't do that shit," replied cornrow. I knew that was true; I hadn't spotted either of them there. "We ain't seen him, alright? And we don't know how the hell his ride got out there. Maybe he got a piece up in here."

"A piece?" Gord asked. "You mean a girl?"

"Yeah."

"Do you know who?"

"No man, I was just speculating on why his ride be parked out back if we ain't seen him. Usually he stop by in the morning to give us a lift but he didn't this morning so we had to take the damn bus to school. Depressing man. I hate the bus."

Gord looked at me and shrugged.

I guess this wasn't going to be as simple as I hoped.

Chapter 33

I lit a cigarette the moment Gord and I left the hellish stairwell.

"That is awful," I said.

"I've seen worse."

"You have?"

"Sure. You wouldn't believe the filth that some people live in right here in the biggest city in one of the most advanced nations in the world, even with the so-called social safety net we've got."

The teens didn't have much else to tell us.

They said that they never knew Bob Junior was into martial arts or knives, that they had only gone to the fights that one time and knew very little about it, that they had been driven in the back of a van so they didn't even know where it was, only that it took more than thirty minutes to get there. They had only met Ray once, the night of that fight. They both agreed the man was a little strange, and cornrow thought he was charged up on methamphetamines or something similar judging by the jittery way he was acting. They said they weren't that close to Bob Junior and that they only started hanging out with him in the last few months and didn't know much about him, only that he had a nice car and liked to play video games. They knew nothing about the cat head. If Bob Junior had done it, he never mentioned a thing to them.

Gord and I left, once he was satisfied that he'd learned everything he could from the teens. He had one of the officers uncuff them and take down all of their pertinent information in case he needed to contact them again.

"So what now?" I asked after we had made the miserable trip down the stairwell.

"I want to go have a little talk with Ray."

"Good idea."

"I'm going to leave someone here to watch the car in case Junior comes back from wherever he's hiding. If the kids are right and he has a girl in this place, he's going to have to come out eventually, no matter how fine she is. Listen, if this thing escalates, we're going to have to take this car in and strip it for evidence."

"And?"

He shook his head. "Christ Lasky, you need to decide if you want to keep your ass out of jail. When we bust Bob Junior and Ray what's-his-name, the car will be looked at. And when it is do you want them to find your tracer?"

"Ohhhh . . . right." Again I felt like a fool.

"Don't you think the detectives will wonder who has the inclination to put a tracer in Bob Junior's car? Hmmm . . . . maybe the nut who was spotted taking pictures of him outside of the school?"

"Okay, okay. So what do I do?"

"No one's around. Pull it. Quick."

I walked to the car and dropped to the ground and reached under and with a hard yank the magnetic seal broke and I stood up with the small tracer in hand.

"Now I need to figure out the best way to approach Ray."

"I told you I already met him, right?"

"No."

"I went in undercover."

He laughed at that. "Undercover! Listen to you."

"I wanted to see what I could dig up so I went into his dojo when I knew Bob Junior was in there and pretended that I wanted to take a class. I told them I worked as hired security for a corporate client, made it seem like a big deal. I said I was John Sherman, personal security specialist."

"John Sherman? Where'd you come up with that?"

"Just popped into my head."

"I need to do some strategizing. You stole that DVD so legally it's useless to us. I need to figure out a good excuse to haul Ray's ass in but I need to do it in such a way that the fact you pulled a B&E never comes up. We got nothing on him right now."

"What about what these kids just told us? They admitted to being at the fight and that Ray was there too."

"Yeah, but only after I asked them outright if they'd been there. That was a poor play on my part. I should have led them to answering that without giving away that I had seen footage of the fight. Any half-witted defense attorney, even some over-worked public defender, will ask me how I knew about the dog fight in the first place. I can't tell them you brought me the DVD without admitting that you broke into his dojo."

"Thanks for watching my back."

"Don't get too sappy. I'd tell them you busted in if it would help the case, but I'm sure the DVD would still be disallowed as evidence even though I wasn't part of the break-in."

"But you knew I was going to do it."

He looked at me, eyes hard. "No I didn't, and don't let me hear you say that again."

"Yeah, yeah, very scary."

"This is serious business, Lasky. Not just people's careers, but also their freedom from prosecution, okay? Best that you forget that you ever set foot inside of that dojo."

But how could I forget those evil haunting eyes that had startled me as I opened the wardrobe shrine?

"Can't you just go and ask him if he's seen Bob Junior? You never know, if there was another fight last night maybe something happened to the kid. Maybe the dog won this time."

"Wouldn't that be great?" He pulled out his cell phone. "Yeah, hey doll, Grossman here. You did? Perfect timing. I was just about to go round him up. Listen, could you have someone check the hospitals for a Robert Linehan Junior? Might have dog bites or knife wounds. Okay, thanks. Okay, sure, it's a date, and the first two rounds are on me, okay?" He disconnected. "Sweet lady. She's pushing fifty but still a shameless flirt. A woman who has defied the ravages of time too, let me tell you." I followed him as he walked toward the Suburban. "She sent me info on Ray. I'm hoping it'll give me something I can use. And in answer to your question, I can't just go ask him if he knows where Bob Junior is since his parents haven't officially reported him missing."

"What if John Sherman were to go ask him?"

"You really like the idea of being this John Sherman, don't you?" he asked and the corner of his mouth raised slightly, suggesting that he was joking, or at least partially joking.

"If you were me, wouldn't you want to be someone else?"

"Christ, Lasky, when did you get to be such a downer?"

Chapter 34

His full name was Raymond James Iger and he had indeed served in the Marines and had seen action during the first Iraq War, the one in the 1990s, the one during which 40% of the soldiers ended up filing claims due to mysterious ailments, or so Gord explained to me. Imagining Ray as suffering from a modern version of post-traumatic stress disorder was not a stretch.

"I saw this guy, Gordo, and he was a strange individual. For one thing, there's no doubt to me that he's on 'roids."

"Even back in high school you always thought everyone was on steroids."

"Everyone was."

"Seriously, Lasky, I ask you: what's so bad about steroids? Aside from the moral issue of breaking the law, what's so bad?"

"Shouldn't that be enough of a reason for you? Didn't you used to be a cop?"

"I know they're illegal but what the hell do the lawmakers know about what's right or wrong in day-to-day life?"

"Christ, Gordo. Were you ever a good cop before you turned out this way?"

"What's it to them if a man wants to take care of himself? Build up some muscle-mass in a hurry?"

I looked at him casually staring at the laptop computer as if the opinion he'd just expressed to me was the most natural thing in the world.

"Are you trying to confess something to me, muscle man?"

"So what makes you think he's juicing?"

"When did you say he left the service?"

"In '97."

"In the photo I saw of him on the wall in his office he was a small, thin or maybe average-sized guy and now a decade later he's a mini-hulk?"

"Ten years is more than enough time to make that sort of transformation, but who knows, maybe he was messed up over there. The whole story of that short war's yet to be written, Lasky. There's got to be a reason why so many vets ended up sick from one thing or another. Our boy Ray served two tours and it seems like he's one of the lucky ones since he hasn't made any claim with Veteran's Administration."

"So how did Ray end up here in Canada?"

"There's nothing about that in this file. He's lived here for four years but he's still a U.S. citizen. He's owned Iger Martial Arts Academy for two years. He pays his taxes like a good boy and has never been arrested here or in the States."

"So none of that helps us, does it? Nothing that we can use to get in there and ask him some questions. We've always got the John Sherman angle but I'm not sure how we can use it."

"Me neither, Lasky. This sneaking around isn't my style. I would much rather kick in the door and shake the bastard until something falls out."

"There's got to be something. Can't you think of some way to engineer a search warrant on the dojo? Once you legally find the DVDs, then—"

"But that's the whole problem. On what basis could I get a warrant? In the eyes of the law, Ray hasn't done anything wrong. Christ, busting in there might even get the Americans involved. Harassing a former marine might not go over so well in Washington. Last thing the force needs right now is to create a diplomatic incident."

His phone rang.

"Grossman." He listened a moment and his face changed. Gone was the casual guy debating a problem with an old chum: he had suddenly returned to being an Emergency Task Force man. "Okay, send it in to me." He turned the computer away from me and tapped away. "Okay, it's coming through. Is the team en route? Did you call Connors and drag his sorry ass out of bed? Good." He started the truck. "On the move." He turned to me. "You gotta get out."

"But my car is back at—"

"Get out." And the look he gave me left me with no option but to comply. I grabbed my bag and got out and he squealed away before I had closed the door.

Chapter 35

It only cost me $7 to take a taxi back to my car. I was tempted to go find another hotel to stay in since a shower sounded wonderful but then I decided I would earn my $500 and try to find Bob Junior. Besides, if I spent another night in the car I would save myself $30, so I thought I would see if I could hold out until tomorrow.

I wanted to find Bob Junior before Gord or his colleagues did since then I would have the chance to ask him a few questions that would help me secure the 10K before he was locked away in police custody.

Though I'd been working with Gord, I harbored no illusions about our relationship. I had no doubt that if he could make this case on his own, he wouldn't mention my name in any way and then would accept the $10,000 reward on behalf of the Sick Kid's Hospital or some other organization instead of giving it to me, the reward's rightful and very deserving owner.

I was going to find out what Bob Junior had been up to in the hours before he disappeared, but before I began work I saw that there was a liquor store just down the street so I drove there and dashed inside for a bottle of malt liquor.

I didn't want to drink my Olde English 800 in the parking lot of the liquor store, so after taking a healthy slug I drove a block to a strip mall and parked as far from the other vehicles as possible.

After draining some more of the malt liquor I lit another cigarette (I admit I was chain-smoking) then activated the tracking device that had been monitoring the tracer I'd planted in Bob Junior's Civic. The tracker is an excellent and extremely expensive piece of equipment that uses GPS technology. This meant that I could stare at the small screen and watch a green line move across the map of Toronto, thus showing me where the Civic had driven before stopping at its current parking spot near the over-flowing dumpsters.

The Civic had not moved since 2:04 a.m, which was when it arrived at the apartment building. Before that it came from the Linehan residence where it had been parked from 11:32 p.m. until 1:48 p.m. The car made only one stop in between teaching his 9:00 class at Ray's dojo and going home and I made note of the address. After taking another mighty belt of the Olde English 800, I drove to the address and saw that it was the bar that Ray and Bob Junior had taken John Sherman and where I had spoken with the beautiful blonde Irene Johansen before the cops hauled me away and ruined the closest thing to a date that I had enjoyed in years. I had watched most of the class leave the dojo together (before I broke in) and it was looking like they weren't on their way to an illegal fight but for post-class drinks.

Then after an hour of talking about the joys of knife-fighting with his students, he went home. After almost two and a half hours he drove to the apartment building. Had he spent that time setting up a date with a girl in the building? Was he waiting for his parents to fall asleep before sneaking out? The fact that the Civic had been at the building all night certainly led credence to the boy's theory that Bob Junior had a girlfriend in the building.

To obtain some more information, I called Bob Senior.

"How are you holding up?" I asked.

"As well as can be expected." I heard Dorothy wailing in the background. "Sorry about that," he said, "I've been trying to convince her to take another tranquilizer but no luck."

"I've been following some leads and—"

"Have you found anything?" he asked quickly.

"Nothing solid yet. I've been trying to track Bob Junior's movements over the past day and I was hoping you would let me ask a couple of questions."

"Shoot."

"What time did Bob Junior get home last night?"

"I'm not sure. Dotty and I were out for dinner with friends. We didn't get home until after 11:00 and there was no sign of him."

The tracker stated that the Civic was there, even if Bob Junior wasn't so I asked, "Was his car there when you got home?"

"No. Not him or his car. We left the house at around 7:00 and he was still there then. He was in his room and nothing seemed out of the ordinary. Now I wish I would have gone down and talked to him to make sure that everything was okay—"

"Do you think he would've had something to tell you?"

"I don't know. Maybe he would have told me he was staying over at a girl's house, like you suggested he might have done."

"Was he home when you arrived from work?"

"I think so. His car was in the driveway. He must have been in his room playing video games. It seems like that's all his generation wants to do . . . play video games like there isn't a whole world out there to play in."

"Thanks, Bob. This has been helpful." And only heightened my suspicions that Bob Senior was keeping things from me. "I'll call you as soon as I have any details."

He thanked me and let me go. Considering how pleasant he had been I wondered if he had popped one or two tranquilizers himself.

Something didn't add up.

Either my tracer was acting up or Bob Senior was wrong

about his son's comings and goings and I trusted my technology a lot more than I trusted either one of the Bobs. I had made a note of the times that Bob Senior had given me and I was just about to compare them to the figures from my tracer to see if they lined up when the phone rang.

It was Gordo.

"We found Bob Junior. He's dead."

Chapter 36

The Scarborough Bluffs extend about 14 kilometers along the shore of Lake Ontario. The erosion of the packed clay cliff-face created the interesting, almost artistic shape of the bluffs, which are 65 meters tall at their highest point. Though there is a good beach nearby and it is always pleasant to take a stroll at the Bluffs on a sunny day, especially if the monarchs at the nearby butterfly sanctuary are taking flight, I have little doubt that a different segment of the populace enjoys the secluded area once the sun goes down.

Robert Linehan Junior was not the first teenage boy to be found dead in the Bluffs and he would not be the last.

I pulled into the parking lot that had ten police vehicles in it including cruisers, Gord's SUV, and a large van that I suspected was for the lab guys. This was the scene at the school on the morning the cat head was discovered amplified ten times over. The only difference was the absence of the media on the scene, though I was sure they would arrive soon. A dead white boy was good news.

It wasn't officer Papineau guarding the entrance to the path leading into the wooded area, which may have explained why I was treated so much better than normal. As soon as I told the uniformed cop my name he told me to continue down the path and that Grossman was waiting for me.

"And you might wanna finish that cigarette before you get there. Lt. Hendrickson hates the smell."

"He's here?"

"Yup."

The old coot. Perfect

Wouldn't you know it that the old man was one of the first officers to see me as I made my way two hundred meters down the trail to where the police were congregated.

"What the hell is he doing here?" Hendrickson asked.

To make it even worse, Sergeant Mike, the cop who'd interrogated me, was there as well. "Haven't you heard? He's Grossman's new pet."

"Watch your step, Mike," Grossman said.

"Or what?"

Grossman stepped close to the man and looked down into his face. "Are you sure you want to see me angry?"

"You gonna turn green and lose your temper and smash everything in sight?"

"I won't turn green."

"No need to fight over me, fellas," I said, chuckling weakly, still not comfortable around so many cops, especially when most of them looked at me without hiding their distaste.

"I brought Lasker here since he's familiar with the victim. He was hired by the boy's father to watch him since the father was worried that the boy was into some bad business—running with a rough crowd, that sort of thing. Maybe he's found something that could give us some leads," Gord suggested.

Detective Mike said, "He claims to be working for Bob Senior. We don't have confirmation of that fact. I called the man myself and he said he never hired a P.I. in his life."

"He did hire me, then he fired me, then just this morning he hired me again when his son went missing. And for your information, he also apologized to me for lying to you."

"Oh really?" Mike laughed. "Am I the only one that thinks that this all sounds delusional?"

"Smells fishy to me," said Lt. Hendrickson, who fixed me with an evil glare from his rheumy eyes.

"You smell like you're drunk too," Mike said.

I had finished off the 40 oz (1.183 liter) bottle of Olde English 800 before getting out of my car, but I only felt a bit buzzed, not terribly drunk. "Not at all. Just had a beer with lunch."

"Right."

"Smells like cigarettes around here too," said the Lieutenant. "Someone smoking?"

"It's this guy," Mike said, pointing at me. "He smells lousy for a lot of reasons. When was the last time you took a shower, Lasker?"

"Look, I came here to help, alright? Why not let me do so without giving me a hard time?"

"He's given me some good tips so far," Gord said in my defense. "That, along with his ongoing work with the family, made me think I should call him in. I want to crack this case as soon as possible. Any objections?"

Gord looked back and forth between the Lieutenant and Sergeant, who was obviously the Lieutenant's man and would go along with him on anything no matter how ridiculous, and neither of them raised any objections.

"Besides," Gord added with a grin, "didn't someone famous say 'keep your friends close and your enemies closer?'"

"That was Sun Tzu in the Art of War," I said.

"No, it's from The Godfather," Mike argued.

"It was in the Art of War first—about 2600 years ago."

"I remember when the godfather said it. He was talking to his men and he said—" Mike then spoke in an atrocious impression of Marlon Brando's signature role. "I keep my friends close and my enemies closer."

The Lieutenant remembered it differently. "Me and the wife saw that movie just last week on the AMC channel and I thought it was Michael the son who told the men that his father used to say 'Keep your friends close and your enemies closer.'"

"Yeah, maybe you're right," Mike said, scratching his head. "Either way, we agree that the Godfather said it, but whether Marlon Brando said it, or whether Al Pacino is quoting him is the only question."

"So maybe the Godfather read the Art of War," I suggested. "It could explain why he managed to do so well and gain so much power."

"You think you're pretty smart don't you?" Mike asked.

"Not really. I just like to read."

"Oh ho!" Mile laughed. "Watch out everybody! We got ourselves a reader!"

I looked at Gord, pleading with him to get me away from Mike before I hit him over the head with one of the sizable branches that lay all around us. "Do you want to show me anything?"

"How about a dead body?"

"Beats the company around here."

We walked away from the group of officers and as soon as I got away from the Lieutenant I lit a cigarette. This was going to be the first dead body I had seen outside of a funeral and I wasn't looking forward to it. I needed nicotine to help calm my frazzled nerves.

The body was a hundred yards farther down the trail on the bank of a shallow stream fed by the city's storm drains. It had been so dry there was no more than half a meter of filthy water flowing slowly toward Lake Ontario.

Bob Junior was lying on his back, his head to the left. His skin was pale and the way it caught the light made it look like it was made of wax. His eyes and mouth were wide open.

The forensics department in white jumpsuits were taking a close look at the body and one of them was photographing the body in detail.

"Someone walking their dog spotted him in the stream there up against the grate," Gord said to me. Then he turned to one of the techs. "Any timeline yet, Errol?"

Errol was a portly man whose physical features were difficult to make out behind the headed suit that kept the investigators from contaminating the scene. "Best guess is twelve to sixteen hours but the fact that he was in the water makes it tough to tell. Birds and scavengers haven't had much of a go at him so that backs up the claim that he hasn't been in there too long."

I looked at my watch. It was 4:30 p.m. now, which meant death occurred between 12:30 a.m. and 4:30 a.m. last night.

I couldn't remember the exact times that his Civic left his parents place, but I thought it was around 2 a.m.

"There's no blood trail," Gord said, "at least not that we've found yet, which makes us think he was killed somewhere else and dumped here."

"Do you know how he died?" I asked.

Gord turned from me to techie. "Errol?"

"From what I can see so far, and this is only preliminary since as you can see he is still clothed so I may be missing wounds, he was killed by an edged weapon here." He pointed to the top of Bob Junior's right shoulder a few centimeters from the neck where a ragged tear was visible in his T-shirt. "A big wound . . . but who knows if that's what killed him. Impossible to say for certain at this point. I'm looking forward to opening him up and seeing what did him in."

"You're looking forward to it?" Gord asked, the disgust clearly written across this face.

"Sure," Errol said with a smile, oblivious to Gord's disdain. "Who doesn't love solving a mystery?"

Chapter 37

"I can't believe the kid's dead."

"Dead and dumped in a polluted little stream like a goddamned stolen shopping cart," Gord said to me.

We were back in the parking lot talking about what to do next. I was smoking another cigarette with trembling hands. The sight of the body had shaken me. I wished I'd bought two bottles of Olde English 800 because if I had, I'd be chugging it right there just to push the waxen image of Bob Junior's corpse from my mind.

"Has anyone contacted his parents yet?" I asked.

"No, but someone will. We've got someone good at that sort of thing who'll be here any minute. We need to get to them before the bloodsuckers in the media do." He pointed up the hill to the television van with the dish on top rolling toward the parking lot. "Speak of the devil and he appears."

"How about I go tell the parents?" I suggested. "Don't you think it would be better to hear it from someone other than a cop?"

"No, Lasky, I think a parent would want to hear this news from a police officer who can then assure them that the full force of the law will find and punish whoever did this terrible thing to their son."

"Okay." I took a deep drag. "I just don't know what I should be doing. I need to do something. I want to help find out who did this to the kid."

"I know." Gord must have seen how upset I was because he said, "I meant what I said down there. You did help a lot on this whole thing."

"Yeah, but none of it helped save the kid."

"You can't think like that. You can't second guess yourself. What if we would have picked him up once we knew he was a dog-killer? Would he still be alive? Sure. He'd be sitting in a cell." He shrugged his broad shoulders. "In this business you'll go crazy if you start asking yourself 'what if?'"

"So what now?"

"We'll take care of things. As for you, I don't know what to say. If you were in this for that reward it's looking like you might be out of luck, that is, if you made Bob Junior as the cat-killer."

I hadn't even thought about that. My precious $10,000! What was I going to do without it? "Goddamn it! I could really use that money right now."

"Tough break, Lasky. Get your license back and then you can start working for a living like the rest of us."

"It's not easy drumming up cases. You got it easy. Someone dies, or some crime happens, you go check it out. Us P.I.s are out there hustling clients, advertising and all of that B.S. It's not easy."

"I bet."

"I don't want to sound callous saying this when there's a body back there."

"You do sound callous, but I understand where you're coming from. We all gotta earn a living. I'm sure your line of work is tough. Hell, I wouldn't want to do it."

Another cop car pulled into the lot and stopped just in front of us.

"Here's our expert at breaking bad news," Gord said.

Great. It was Officer Papineau.

"What the hell is he doing here?" she asked, jerking a thumb in my direction as she stepped out of the cruiser.

"Good to see you too, Officer Papineau."

"He's been helping me out. He's been working with the Linehan family so I thought I'd bring him down."

"What do you see in this guy, Grossman?"

"Hey!" I said, "I'm standing right here!"

"Yeah? You should see the way I talk about you when you're not around."

"He's alright," Gord said. "But the way everyone else on the force seems to hate him is starting to make me question my judgment."

"What? You know me, Gord! You know I am a stand-up guy! What about all those days of glory out there on the gridiron?" I asked.

"Oh no . . ." Papineau moaned. "Don't tell me that this is a sports thing . . ."

"High school all-stars, both of us," I said. "City champs."

"And provincial champs in football one year," Gord added, "and I went to the nationals in wrestling every year."

"What is it with you men and sports? You're on a team together and it's like you're bonded for life or something."

"All kidding aside," Gord said, "I just want to close this case as soon as we can and if Lasker can help, it's worth bringing him in."

She looked me up and down again and from her expression it was obvious that she wasn't impressed by what she was seeing. "If you say so. Tell me about this kid."

"Robert Linehan Junior," Gord began. "Went to Winston Churchill High and we have reason to suspect that he had something to do with the cat head."

Papineau turned to me with a smile. "I'm still laughing over that line about you getting hired by mice to investigate the cat." Her and Gord laughed and I nodded with an expression that I hoped showed how unimpressed I was.

"Yeah, hilarious," I said.

"Errol thinks that Bob Junior was killed sometime during the night, most likely somewhere else and then dumped in the stream, where he lay for twelve hours or so before a jogger found him. Cause of death could be a wound to the neck, but he's not sure. We know that Bob Junior was mixed up in some rough stuff—underground fighting and who knows what else—and his parents must have had some idea that he was going bad since they hired Lasker here to tail him."

"Were you watching him last night when he was killed?" she asked me.

"No. I was fired by then. I got re-hired this morning when Bob Senior saw that his son had gone missing."

The suspicion was plainly written on her face. "Funny timing, Grossman, don't you think it's strange that this guy is around this kid and the cat head? Doesn't that ring any alarm bells in that bald head of yours?"

"He's okay, Papineau," he said sternly, "so drop it, okay?"

She just shrugged.

"So you've got the Linehan address, right?" he asked.

She said she did. I got the feeling that she didn't like being snapped at by the big man.

"Listen, I know he isn't your favorite guy, but how about you take Lasker with you when you break the news."

"No way! This isn't a job for a civilian!"

"He's working for them and he knows them. From what he told me the parents are pretty broken up over their missing son so having a familiar face there might help, okay? Now get moving before the press get their cameras up and rolling."

"Fine," she said, and then turned to me. "But if you piss me off I'm going to hit you with pepper spray, then Taser you, then shoot you, understand?"

"Um . . . I'm not sure I feel too comfortable going with you under those circumstances since I seem to piss you off without even trying and if—"

"Just get in the car, Lasky," Gord said.

And I did.

Chapter 38

"I bet you don't have much experience sitting in the front seat of police cruisers," Officer Papineau said, suggesting, of course, that I had plenty of experience being arrested and being put in the rear seat.

"Not in the front seat of cruisers, but in my younger days I certainly gained a lot of experience in the backseat of my trusty Dodge—"

"Please . . . you're making me ill."

"You really do know how to flatter a guy, don't you?"

"I don't need to flatter men. Wearing this uniform is like a magnet to the opposite sex. There's no shortage of men in this city that get a thrill from the idea of dating a cop."

"Perhaps it's your charm that wins them over."

"Maybe it is," she replied, ignoring my sarcasm.

"But in all honesty I bet you're a good looking woman under all of that."

My face nearly went through the windshield when she slammed on the brakes. As it was I was nearly strangled by the seatbelt. Once the car had come to a stop she said, "What did you just say to me?"

"I-I-I just meant to say you're a good looking woman but that the uniform and bullet-proof vest . . . well . . . looking at you one sees a cop first and the woman second, you know?"

"When you look at me I don't want you to see a woman first second or ever. All I want you to see is a cop who would love to kick your ass out of this cruiser right now."

"Okay." I held up my hands in surrender. "I didn't mean anything by it."

After glaring at me for a few seconds, she slowly pulled away. "You don't know the shit a woman goes through on this job and it's comments like that that I don't need. Got my fill of that back when I was a rookie and every horny cop in the city would make a play."

"I'm sorry," I said sincerely. "It can't be easy."

"Don't be sorry. I'm just telling you why I need you to cool it with those kind of statements before I am forced to pepper spray you then—"

"Then Taser me, then shoot me. I got it."

"Good. Don't forget it."

A few minutes later we pulled up in front of the Linehan residence. When I saw the Johnson residence (no sign of Ms. Johnson unfortunately), I asked Papineau, "Do you know if anyone ever showed the Johnson's a picture of the cat that was found in front of Winston Churchill?"

"Not that I know. Why would they?" We climbed out and began walking toward the house.

"I think that the cat belonged to that house there," I said, pointing, "and I was wondering if anyone ever confirmed it."

"You'll have to ask someone else. I'm just a uniform, Lasker. Not like I know about every detail of every case."

"Okay." Was there bitterness in her words? Was Officer Papineau tired of her uniform? Was she tired of taking orders from Grossman and others like him?

She rang the doorbell.

"Let me do the talking," she said.

I was happy to do so. Seeing the boy's body was bad enough. I know I had volunteered to break the news, but as I stood there in front of the white door listening to the bell ding-donging inside I felt my knees go weak and I felt dizzy all of a sudden.

"Are you alright?" Papineau asked, "You're pale as a sheet."

I nodded weakly. I didn't want to say anything that might cause her impression of me to fall even further. There she was looking strong and confident and it took all of my resolve to not ask to wait in the car. "I'm okay."

The door opened.

Dorothy Linehan stood before us in a housecoat, looking even more distraught than when I had seen her that morning.

As soon as she saw the uniformed officer and my pained pale expression, she brought her hand to her mouth and began shaking uncontrollably. She took a step back from the doorway.

"No, no, no, no, no, no." Tears rolled down her face and she shook her head with each word. "No, no, no, no, no."

"Mrs. Linehan," Papineau said, "I am so sorry to have to tell you—"

But before Papineau could finish telling the woman the worst news any parent could hear, she fainted and collapsed to the floor with a thump.

Chapter 39

Dorothy Linehan was sitting on the couch with Officer Papineau on her right, who was doing her best to console her. Dotty had refused the offer for an ambulance when she regained consciousness moments after collapsing. She held several tissues in her hands and used them to wipe tears away.

"H-how?"

"Are you sure you wouldn't rather wait for your husband to come back?"

"He wanted to go to the office, just needed to go to the office," she said, her voice thick with anger, "so let him stay there. J-just tell me how he died."

"We won't know until the post-mortem is completed," she said, "but foul play is suspected."

"Oh god . . ." Dorothy began to wail and the sound ripped at my heart. The poor, poor woman.

I had, after Papineau said it was a good idea, called Bob Senior on his cell but it had gone straight through to his mobile. Not sure of what to say, I simply said it was extremely urgent that he call me ASAP.

"What kind of man goes to the office when his boy is . . ." There was a new round of tears. "I was going to say 'when his boy is missing' b-but Bobby isn't m-missing anymore, is he?"

It was heart-wrenching to watch the poor woman breaking down and I wanted to do something, anything to help her. "Is there anyone I can call for you? Anyone that you'd like to have come over?"

"No, no. All of my family lives in Kingston and I don't think I could bear to see them right now. Do you get along with your family?" she asked Papineau.

"Not as well as I should. I have two sisters and sisters can be . . . difficult."

"I only have one, but that's more than enough." Dorothy seemed to be getting a hold of herself, though it was probably just a brief reprieve, since in my own experience, the worst heartache hits hard then fades like a tide, then hits again as hard or harder than before and goes on and on and on.

"So you understand," Dorothy said. "If she was here you know she would turn this whole thing around so it was so terrible that she should lose a nephew when it's me who . . ." Again came the tears. Dorothy leaned into Papineau, who put her arms around the woman.

"I'll be just outside," I whispered to Papineau, who nodded in response.

I sat on a bench on their veranda and lit a cigarette, and I could hear a wail rise out of Dorothy. Poor woman. To get such news and being alone with a cop while your husband works in the office. What kind of husband would leave his wife when she was in such a state? I had seen her that morning and if I was married to her I would never have left her alone with her heartache and worry. Then again, I wasn't head of DMC industries with all of the pressures that came with owning and operating such an enterprise. Maybe something came up that required his attention; something more important that being there for his distraught wife.

"Hello, Mr. Lasker."

"Oh, hello, Ms. Johnson."

I must have been lost in somber reverie to not have noticed the beautiful woman walking from her house next door.

"Is everything okay? I could hear Dorothy crying even though I was in my back yard."

What to say to her? I had no idea how one handles situations like this. "Are you friendly with her?"

"Of course. I wouldn't say that we are friends, but we certainly are neighborly. Is she alright?"

"I'm not sure if I should be telling you this but I will." I spoke the next part quietly, "Bob Junior is dead."

She brought her hand to her mouth. "What? I don't believe it."

"Murder by the looks of it."

"Oh my God . . ." She sat on the bench next to me and, like me, spoke in hushed tones. "I-I don't know what to say. Murdered?"

I nodded.

She pointed at my cigarette. "Could you give me one of those?"

I pulled out the pack and she took one and I lit it for her.

"I quit two years ago but . . ." She shrugged. "I didn't really know him but he seemed like a good kid."

"It's a sad day."

"When did it happen?"

"Late last night. Past midnight is the best guess."

"Oh poor Bob—Senior I mean. Not just about losing his son, but it can't be easy on him considering what I saw last night."

"Which was?"

"They had a fight. This was late. Must have been past 12:00 since I had just finished watching an old CSI. They were yelling so loud that I could hear it from inside my place. If that was the last time they spoke . . ." She shook her head. "Hard enough to lose a family member, but I imagine it would be even harder if the last words were harsh ones."

Remembering the heated exchange I had witnessed in the driveway of that house a few days earlier I asked, "Was it unusual for them to argue?"

"Well . . . it wasn't the first time I'd heard them. This one seemed worse though. It went on and on, and then I guess Bob Junior got into his car and roared down the street and things were quiet after that."

"Do you remember what time he left?"

"Not exactly. Before 12:30 I think. It might have been later."

"Did you see him get into the car?"

"No, but I'm sure the whole neighborhood heard him, considering the noise that car of his makes. Roars like a jet."

I would need to look at my notes to see what time my tracer had the Civic leaving this place. The car went straight to the apartment building and the two boys said that they hadn't seen Bob Junior that night. Were they lying or did he have some other reason for being at that building?

My phone rang. It was Bob Senior.

"Hello, Bob," I said, wondering how I was going to handle this call.

"I have great news!" he said in an excited voice. "The Bombardier deal went through just this minute! So you can tell your mysterious source who told you that it was a done deal when it wasn't, that the deal has been signed and finalized! It's not something I liked to talk about, but DMC was in trouble and if we hadn't—"

"Bob—"

"It's a great day for the company, Derek, a great day! This work will see us through the next year or more and who knows what the future will hold. It's all about that first big step and this is indeed a huge step for DMC!"

"Bob—"

"All of the boys down here are excited about the news and one of the fellas has broken out the beer to celebrate."

"Bob, I have news."

"You found Bob Junior?"

After a brief pause I said, "Yes."

"Good. Then this day is getting better and better. Thanks for letting me know." And with that, he disconnected. I called him back and was put through to his voicemail. I told him to call his wife and that there was something she needed to talk about and that maybe he should come home now.

"How is he taking it?" Ms. Peterson asked.

"He doesn't know about it yet. He's too busy celebrating a big business deal he just signed with your husband."

"Really?"

"You didn't know about it?"

"No. Neither of them like to talk about business to me." She smiled weakly. "You know how protective men can be. They like to guard their secrets, don't they?" She took a final draw of the cigarette before tossing it to the lock stones and crushing it beneath her foot.

Chapter 40

The lovely Ms. Peterson had gone back to her place by the time Bob Senior's SUV rolled into the driveway. The previous day, the idea of sitting on a bench smoking cigarettes with Ms. Peterson would have sounded like bliss, but today was marred by the image of Bob Junior's waxen face staring into nothingness. It was certainly not the time for playful flirtation. She sat with me for a few minutes after finishing her cigarette then said she should go home.

By the time Bob Senior got there I had smoked five more cigarettes and I could still hear intermittent sobs from inside of the house.

There was a large smile on Bob's face as he stepped out of his vehicle and I thought there was a weave in his walk as he moved toward me. Just how many beers had he downed during the celebration at DMC?

"Derek! I didn't expect you to be here! How the hell are you?"

"Have a seat, Bob."

"How about I go inside and grab us a couple of cold ones first?"

"Have a seat. I need to talk to you."

He sat down heavily and I could indeed smell the beer on him. "What's up?" he asked amiably.

"I don't know how to say this except to blurt it out. It wasn't me who found Bob Junior, it was the cops. He's dead."

"What? Is this a joke?"

"No joke. It looks like murder, Bob. I'm sorry."

The smile was still on his face, as if the shock had locked it there, but there was pain in his eyes and slowly the smile melted. "Murder? Who would murder my son? Do they know who did it?"

"I don't think so."

He leaned forward and put his face in his hands. "Oh my god. How did this happen? When?" he asked suddenly. "When did they say this happened?"

"Late last night. Sometime after midnight is their best guess."

"What?" He looked at me, his red eyes wet with tears. "But he was home until 12:00 and he went out just after we . . . we had a talk about some things." His face twisted and the tears came in earnest. "I argued with him, Derek. I argued with him and then he got in his car and drove away and . . . and then you said that shortly after that . . . someone . . . but who? Who would do that to a boy?"

There was no shortage of people in this world who would kill for reasons that the sane members of the human race found difficult to comprehend. What motivates someone to take the life of another? The list was impossibly long.

"I don't know," I said, "but the police are going to do everything they can to find out, I'm sure of that. They've got their best people on it. They wanted me to assure you and your wife that they won't rest until they find who did this. An officer is inside with Dorothy right now and—"

That caught his attention. "Someone's in there talking to her?"

"Comforting her, yes."

He stood up quickly and sprinted to the door, pulled it open and rushed inside. I followed him into the living room, where Papineau was still sitting next to Dorothy, cups of tea on the table in front of them.

"What is this? What the hell are you doing in here?" he asked Papineau.

Before she could answer, Dorothy leapt to her feet,

bumping the coffee table, knocking both cups of tea onto the carpet, and screamed at her husband.

"How dare you! You bastard! How dare you waltz in here and talk to her like that! She's been good to me! Her uniform is wet with my tears, Bob!"

"What I want to know, Dotty, is why are you sitting here talking to the police?"

Dorothy was shaking. "I-I'm not talking to the police! This kind woman is consoling me over the death of my son! Do you even care? Do you care that my son is dead?"

"Of course I care! He was my boy too, Dotty!"

"Then why would you speak like this? You just had to go to the office and leave me alone to get this news! We couldn't reach you on the phone and—"

"I had no choice! I had to go to the office or risk losing this entire deal!"

"Oh yes! Your precious deal!"

"This deal is going to keep us going for a long time, Dotty!"

"But our son is dead!"

"I-I know."

"And you weren't here for me!"

"And I'm sorry for that but you need to understand that sometimes business needs—"

"Your business! Your business! What about your son? What about your wife?"

I glanced over at Papineau and our eyes met. We were both uncomfortable being witness to this domestic scene but didn't know how to extricate ourselves from the situation. It occurred to me that we may need to stay and make sure things didn't escalate to a dangerous level.

Bob sighed. "I know, Dotty. I wish I didn't have to go. I really do. I-I hate that I wasn't here with you when these people came by with the terrible news. I'm sorry. I'll make it up to you somehow."

"No, Bob! You can never make it up to me! Never! You abandoned me just like you abandoned your son!"

"I didn't—"

"You sure as damned well did! I heard you last night! I heard you arguing with him!"

"Yes, we did argue, but remember, you took a sleeping pill along with your medication so what you think you heard may not be real, you know that."

"Don't give me that nonsense! I know what I heard!"

He took a step toward his wife and she stepped back. "Don't touch me! I want you out of this house! Go back to your business! Your precious business!"

"We need to be together now. Our son is—"

"I know what our son is, Bob! I know! I knew while you were at the office doing whatever it is that was so damned important!"

"I was making the biggest deal of my life, Dotty!"

"While your son lay dead in a creek."

He took a shuddering breath. "And I'm sorry for that. I am so sorry but I had no way of knowing. I thought he was at a friend's place or with that girlfriend that you kept secret from me. I thought he would come waltzing in with some excuse about where he'd been and then we could yell at him and tell him that he put us through hell and then things would go back to the way—"

"I heard you arguing! You drove him away!"

"I-I didn't . . . well . . . oh, Dotty! I wish I never had that fight with him, I really do. Oh god! Maybe if we didn't, he wouldn't have driven off and . . . g-gotten into trouble. But wishing it won't change things."

Dotty slumped to the sofa and began sobbing. "You drove him away. You drove my son away."

He sat next to her and this time she didn't recoil from

him, but laid her head in his lap and sobbed. He looked up at the two of us.

"Could you both leave? We need to be alone now."

Papineau asked Dorothy, "Is that what you want?"

Dorothy just cried without answering.

Papineau pulled out a business card and put it on the coffee table. "Call me anytime, day or night, okay?"

"Thank you both for coming," Bob said. "I trust you can show yourselves out?"

As we walked across the yard toward her cruiser, Papineau said, "What a fucking piece of work that guy is."

And I could not disagree.

Chapter 41

"So what do you think?" I asked Papineau as we pulled away from the Linehan house and drove through the lovely residential neighborhood on our way back to the Bluffs.

"About what?"

"Didn't that situation seem strange to you?"

"Of course it did," she said. "They just found out that their son was murdered."

"But how do you explain Bob's reaction?"

"No matter how many times I'm forced to break the news I'll never get used to it. People always react in strange and unexpected ways. Sometimes they break down like she did and sometimes they get angry like he did. Sometimes they do something else. The human psyche reacts in strange ways to that kind of thing, Lasker."

"But why was he so upset that Dorothy was talking to you?"

"Because he's an asshole? Because he's in shock? Because he feels guilty about not being there for her? Who knows? Okay, to be honest, it felt strange to me too but all I can do is pass on the information to the investigating officers and trust them to run with it."

"Can I say something and you promise you won't get mad?"

"I won't promise, but I will try to restrain myself."

"You're wasted in a uniform, Officer Papineau. You should be out there in a suit investigating crimes instead of guarding crime scenes and breaking the news to grieving families."

She looked at me with suspicion.

"It's just an observation," I said. "I've seen the men this city makes detectives and they could use a few more people like you to help them out."

"As a matter of fact I'm studying for my detective's test right now. I take it in two weeks."

"Good. I know you'll do well."

She was not very talkative during the brief drive back to the Bluffs, which was not surprising considering the raw emotional drama that we'd both witnessed.

There was still a large police presence in the parking lot, as well as three media vehicles, each with crews milling around the officers hoping to get more information. There was no sign of Gord's Suburban.

"Thanks for the ride, Officer Papineau," I said as I stepped out of the cruiser that she had pulled in front of my car. "And good luck on the test."

"Listen," she said, "if you see me again, you can call me Barbara."

I bent back into the car and smiled. "Thanks. And you can call me Derek." I was expecting her to put the car back into gear and tell me to get the hell away from the cruiser before she inflicted violent death upon me, but she just sat there with her hands on the wheel, looking forward. I asked, "Are you okay?"

"Sometimes I just get so tired," she said quietly.

"I know how you feel."

"That woman today, Dorothy, how many times can I break that kind of news before it starts to get to me? They say I'm good at it just because I'm a woman. They won't say that to my face but I damned well know that's why they order me to do it. Just because of my gender I'm supposed to be able to handle this sort of thing?"

"I don't know how you do it," I said, "You must be very strong."

✳

She laughed softly. "If only you knew how wrong you are." Finally she put the car into gear. "Take care of yourself, Derek."

"You too, Barbara."

I closed the door and she pulled out of the lot.

I got into my car and called Gord but he didn't pick up. I left a message on his voicemail saying that I was back in my car after talking to the Linehan's and was available if he needed help with anything. I also told him about Bob Senior's strange reaction and that I could talk to him about it if he wanted. After leaving the message I was worried that I'd sounded desperate. Hell, I was desperate.

I sat at the wheel smoking a cigarette (I had nearly emptied the pack) and watched the reporters from every major network recording their bits for the evening news.

What now? I wondered.

The $10,000 was looking like a lost dream and Bob Senior would have no further need for me. I had most of his $500 in my wallet but had no leads on how to earn any more money. The past days had been exciting for me and I had felt useful for the first time in recent memory. Being part of this investigation had been restorative. I had felt alive. There was no denying that I had seen more action in the past few days than I'd seen in months, and that the adventure had kept the worst of the blues away. The problem was except for the few hundred dollars in my wallet (and how long could that last me?), I was no further along than when Bob Senior first called me and asked me to tail his son. Perhaps my parting words with Officer Papineau—Barbara—had brought me down. But still the question I had to answer was, What now for Derek Lasker?

Chapter 42

Over the next twenty-four hours I tried to look to the future with optimism, and to see everything that I had been a part of as the start of a new and positive period in my life. I was going to turn it all around; take better care of myself and to put more effort into my business. Spending time with Gord even had me thinking that I should try to reconnect with more of my old friends that I had let slip away over the years. Maybe being around them would help me feel better about myself and that would in turn help every other aspect of my life. I was possessed with such positive thinking!

I checked into another motel that was no better than Hasid's place. I'd briefly debated going back to his motel and trying to convince the man that I was not the bad person that the cops had painted me as and that I had in fact been working with them and that the whole affair was a big misunderstanding. But as much as I liked Hasid and his family, I decided against it. He said he never wanted to see me again and I had to respect that, no matter how much it hurt my pride. Maybe once I really turned myself around I could go back and take his family out to dinner or do something nice for them. Buy them some flowers to jazz up the property or something like that.

As soon as I got into the room I took a long hot shower. I'd stopped by a drug store before booking into the motel to buy some toiletries: shampoo, conditioner, deodorant, shaving supplies, nail clippers, a comb, a new toothbrush, and mouthwash. I must have spent over an hour in that bathroom but by the time I left the room I looked and felt great, better than I had in months.

I hopped in my car and splurged on a $16 Superclips haircut that ended up looking pretty good. It was a bit shorter than I would have liked but it was still an improvement over the shaggy mop that now lay in piles around the barber's chair.

Next I took myself out to a pub and ordered a shepherd's pie and drank a couple of pints while watching the Blue Jays beat the Red Sox, 7-6, in a thrilling game. It made for a fine way to pass a few hours and I went back to my room feeling quite good about the world and my place in it. Anytime a stray thought about the unknown and scary future drifted into my mind I pushed it away because I didn't want to deal with it.

I was back in my room in time to watch the 11:00 news and I saw the correspondent's pieces that were recorded earlier that day in the Bluffs. Watching them was an interesting experience, as if I was part of the news. I was beginning to understand why Gord loved being on tele-vision so much. I was kicking myself for not spending more time in that parking lot and ingratiating myself with the reporters and convincing one of them that I was worthy of an interview. Then I could have plugged Lasker Invest-igations on the news, and surely that would have helped business. I missed a good opportunity, which may have explained why Lasker Investigations was all but dead. You could be certain that a business wiz like Bob Linehan Senior never missed an opportunity to increase DMC's profile, even if it did mean leaving his wife alone at home when she needed him most. At least he'd made enough money to afford a lovely house with a view of Lake Ontario instead of living in a string of lousy motels with no real prospects for making a living once the last of the money was spent. In a bid to stay positive, I pushed those negative thoughts away.

A lovely reporter with thick shiny black hair spoke to the camera in a well-practiced tone. "A grisly discovery today at the Scarborough Bluffs as the body of a seventeen year old high school boy has been found in a drainage creek. Police report that foul play is suspected."

The footage cut to the delightfully abusive Detective Mike, speaking from a podium with the seal of the Toronto Police behind him. Lieutenant Hendricks was also in the shot, just to Mike's left.

"We are following several clues and have a suspect in custody."

That statement caused me to perk up.

"Who is the suspect?" the reporter asked.

My question exactly.

"We can't comment on that at this time."

"Did the victim know the suspect or was this a random killing?"

That was a good question too, and not one that I would have thought to ask. Mike looked over at Lt. Hendricks, who gave a slight nod.

Mike then answered, "The suspect knew the victim. That's all we can say for now. Thank you."

The reporter wrapped it up and back in the studio the newscaster started talking about high gas prices and that oil had hit another all-time high.

I called Gord and left yet another message, asking him about the suspect. As I hung up I wondered: Who was it? Not knowing was infuriating. I had some idea of who it might be and wanted to know if my suspicions were correct. I hadn't heard from Gord since we parted ways at the Bluffs that afternoon and being left out of the loop was frustrating. I did my best not to think about it. I was a civilian and probably had no right to know the things I did. I was lucky to have been given the access that I had. Maybe telling me

details at this point would hurt their case or something.
Who knows? I only hoped that I had helped the case in
some way and that, I must be honest here, my help would
in turn help me get some cases of my own.

It had been an active couple of days and I hadn't slept
terribly well the previous night (how well can one sleep in
the backseat of a car?), so after reading a bit more of
Macbeth, I fell asleep with the thoughts of that disloyal and
murderous husband and wife going through my mind. And
in spite of murders both real and literary, I slept a sound
and dreamless sleep.

Chapter 43

The good news came later the next afternoon.

The media had nothing new on the Bob Junior case and the police had yet to release the name of their suspect. And I still hadn't heard back from Gord. I resisted the urge to leave another message since I'd left three the previous day. I felt that was more than enough. If he didn't want to talk to me so be it. It appeared that Gord had no further use for my services and I admit that I was thinking poorly of him and the way he cut me off just as the case was coming together, but my opinion of him changed completely when my mobile rang at 3:30.

"Is this Lasker Investigations?" asked a man's voice.

"Yes it is," I said, straightening up in bed, tossing the battered Penguin edition of Crime and Punishment to the floor. "Derek Lasker speaking."

"I'd like to hire you for a case."

"I see." I looked around the room trying to find a pen or pencil and a piece of paper. I was completely unprepared! I finally found a pen and was ready to write on the borders of the Toronto Star that I had purchased that morning. "And your name?"

"Duncan Morley."

"And what can Lasker Investigations do for you, Mr. Morley?"

"I'd rather not talk about it over the phone. It's a bit of a delicate issue."

"Of course. Discretion is our specialty."

"I thought you were the surveillance specialists?"

Had he seen the sign?

"Discretion and surveillance are both specialties of ours," I said, hoping that it didn't sound as lame as I suspected it did. "How did you hear about us?"

"Gordon Grossman told me you were the best."

That struck me by surprise. "Really? When did he tell you that?"

"This morning."

"So you're a friend of his?"

"Look, time is a factor, so could I meet you? We can talk about how we both know Gordon later, okay?"

"Sure. Fine. Whatever you say. When and where would you like to meet?"

The time was right now and the where was behind a strip mall not too far from my motel.

"Why around back?" I asked him.

"I don't want to be seen with you," he replied. "It'll all make sense when I tell you my situation."

"Okay, I understand. Like I said, discretion is our specialty."

"You put the private in private investigator, huh?" He laughed at his poor attempt at humor and I was hungry enough for a case that I laughed along with him.

"Good one, Mr. Morley."

I said I would be there in half an hour.

"Could you make it sooner? I'm in a hurry to meet you."

"Okay. Fifteen minutes?"

"Better. And another thing, don't tell anyone that you're meeting with me, okay? I need to keep things secret for the time being. Like I said, it will all make sense once I explain my situation."

"If you're willing to pay my fee then you can set the rules, Mr. Morley." God, being a business owner really did mean kissing ass sometimes. It was quite embarrassing.

"See you soon," he said before he disconnected.

I sprang from the bed thrilled that my luck had changed.

Things were really beginning to turn around for me!

Working with the police may not have helped me get the $10,000, but if Gordon steered a few cases my way, it could help reinvigorate my career! As I moved around the room getting ready for my meeting I was almost giddy with excitement.

As I rushed out to my car I called Gord's phone and left another message.

"I know I've already left a ton of messages for you and I know you must be busy but I just wanted to thank you for recommending me to Duncan Morley. I appreciate your faith in me, buddy. I owe you a pint of beer."

I hung up and got into my car and ten minutes later I pulled into the strip mall, one of many that lined the main streets of Scarborough. This one was worse than most, with most of the stores abandoned. There was a Salvation Army Thrift Store at the far end and even that had a large sign in the window that read Closing Out Sale! I thought that after the meeting I would duck in there and take a look at the bookshelf since you could get paperbacks for fifty cents, even less if they were on sale due to the closing.

I drove around to the back just as Mr. Morley had asked me to do. It was indeed a good place to have a clandestine meeting since it looked like no one had been back there for years. There was a decent collection of old beds, mattresses and other junk that had presumably been tossed out the back of the Thrift Store and forgotten about.

I pulled to a stop and killed my engine. There was no sign of another car, of Duncan Morley, or anyone else for that matter. Judging by my Casio digital watch, I was three minutes early, which made me smile. I was feeling like a very efficient businessman. Early even for a last minute appointment! Things were truly looking up for me.

I stepped out of my car and sat on the hood and puffed away on a cigarette. I really had been smoking a lot lately.

How had I managed to go from barely smoking at all (due to lack of funds), to smoking like a chimney in a matter of days?

Terrible things, cigarettes. Some said they were the most addictive thing in the world and that quitting nicotine was even harder than kicking heroin. I didn't quite agree with that because I'd known friends who'd been forced to kick heroin and it wasn't a pretty sight.

I was pondering these random thoughts when I heard a noise from behind me, which I assumed was my future client, Duncan Morley, but before I could turn around to greet him, something hard struck me in the back of the head and launched me into the pile of bed frames and mattresses, knocking me out cold.

Chapter 44

Blood.

As I drifted back from the void of unconsciousness I realized that it was blood I was tasting. Funny, since I was having a dream about my mouth being full of pennies. I was a child trying to buy a popsicle and I stood at the counter in the corner store near where I grew up and I leaned forward, opened my mouth and pennies began to fall out as payment for the frozen treat. I really wanted that creamsicle and it would have done wonders to combat the foul taste in my mouth.

"Well, well! Look who's waking up!"

Before my eyes could focus I could smell something spicy-sweet. Incense. I blinked a few times to clear my eyes, which were stinging quite badly, and I saw that I was in Ray's dojo and that Ray was leaning forward and smiling as he stared into my face.

"Good morning sunshine!" he said, his eyes wild.

I was sitting in a chair, unable to move. I looked down and saw that packing tape bound my legs and torso tight to the chair and my arms were fastened behind my back. I'd been immobilized by what must have been hundreds of meters of tape.

"What's happening?" I asked, still groggy.

"I know about you," he hissed, "I know what you're up to."

"What are you talking about?"

He straightened up and laughed. "You're not as smart as you think you are and not as careful as you should be."

"Listen, Ray, whatever this is about surely we can—"

For a man so hugely muscled, he moved fast, so fast that it seemed that I felt the punch to the stomach before my eyes registered that he had moved. The pain was intense and made all the worse by the tape that prevented me from hunching over. I could feel a throbbing inside of me and I wondered if something had ruptured.

"Shut up!" he screamed. "This is no negotiation you piece of shit! You're a prisoner of war!"

"War? What war?"

"You tell me, Derek Lasker, or John Sherman, or whatever the hell your name is."

Fear was beginning to grow in me as I watched Ray pacing in front of me, his face red and the veins on his neck swollen up and looking like steel cables beneath the skin.

"My name's Derek Lasker."

"So you say, so you say. Answer me this, mystery man, who are you working for?"

"No one. Not anymore. I was working for Bob Linehan Senior but once they found his son there was nothing for me to do."

"We both know that working for him was just a cover. Aren't you a little curious about how your pathetic charade fell apart, Mr. Who-ever-you-are?"

"I didn't mean to deceive you. I was just doing my job and didn't mean anything—"

"Yeah, yeah. Just doing my job. Just following orders, huh? I was a soldier and us soldiers have been using that defense since ancient times! People always got a choice, mystery man! Free choice is what makes us human! It's what separates us from dogs, and you're not a dog, are you? Are you?"

"N-no." My fear was increasing with the intensity of Ray's words. He was speaking with such passion that he was spitting with each word.

"So let me tell you about how badly you screwed up, soldier. Let me tell you how your scheme went fubar."

"F-fubar?"

Ray smiled and leaned close, close enough that I could smell his spearmint breath. If I lived I would never be able to chew spearmint gum again. "Fucked up beyond all recognition."

"Sounds like a pretty good description of my life."

"I agree," he said with a smile. He had quickly flipped from rage to levity and that instability scared me as well. "And people think the military don't know what they're doing. It took brains to come up with a word that so perfectly sums up the modern world, don't you think?"

"Definitely."

"Does the name Irene ring a bell?"

"No."

"Sexy blonde? Nice curves? Likes to drink?"

The woman I had shared drinks with at the bar after pretending to be John Sherman with Ray and Bob Junior. "Right. Irene Johansen."

"Was that her last name? I never asked. I did her in the parking lot, can you believe that? Right there in the backseat of my SUV. She's a dirty girl but you never got the chance to find out did you? The cops came in and hauled you away and she told me all about it. She'd seen us talking and said that you came back in and pulled something from under the table where we had been sitting." Ray grabbed me by the throat and held it, not terribly tight, but just on the verge of pain. "What did you take from under the table? A bug? Why were you recording us?"

"I didn't take anything from the table. I just forgot my keys and—"

"Liar!" He squeezed my throat so tightly that I saw stars and nearly blacked out. He wasn't just constricting my windpipe, but the blood flow to my brain. It was a pain greater than anything I had ever experienced. "Tell me the truth or I will kill you slow! So slow that you'll beg to die!"

"Okay," I squeaked from beneath his grip, "It was a bug."

He let go and I gasped for breath and the blood flowing back into my head began to throb in my ears.

"Why did you plant a bug?"

"I was following Bob Junior. I thought that he killed that cat and put the head in front of his high school. I was after the reward."

His laughter clearly indicated that he didn't believe me. "So now you're a bounty hunter?"

"I'm a private investigator that needed that $10,000."

"So there I was back at the bar later that night, chatting up the sexy and half-drunk Irene and she tells me that she watched my friend get hauled out by two cops. 'What friend?' I ask her and she says, 'Derek Lasker, the private investigator.' Now at first I didn't think too much about it since I figured a man will say anything to score a piece of ass but later on I started thinking about it again. I remembered that I saw you hanging around the dojo watching me that day before you came in here."

"I was tailing Bob Junior."

"Shut up!"

"Okay, sorry, please don't hit me again," I begged.

"So I saw you watching me and then the next day you just show up at the dojo with this story about how you work security for some bigwig hush-hush client. You know something? As soon as I saw you walk in, I knew you were a snake. Call it a marine's instinct. Still I was willing to just let it go 'cause what was I going to do? I had to wait for you to make a play, right? I tried to find a John Sherman in the city and there were too many of them to narrow down my search. I still got some friends south of the border but they couldn't tell me if a John Sherman worked security at the last G7 meeting, which is a pretty big hole in their security as I'm sure you'll agree."

"That does surprise me," I said, my mind whirling with pain and confusion and panic.

"I was willing to let it go until I had a surprise visitor yesterday. Can you guess who?"

"No."

"None other than your pal, Bob Linehan Senior. He stopped by in the morning looking very tense and asking me if I had seen his son. I told him I hadn't seen him since the night before when he taught his class. He then told me that he had been worried about his son, so worried that he'd hired a private investigator to follow him."

"See? I told you!"

"He even told me that he had found you from a sign posted outside of Wong's Chinese."

"We're the surveillance specialists."

He laughed but his voice betrayed no trace of humor, like he was laughing because he felt it was the right thing to do at that moment. "That's right. And the poor quality of your sign as well as Bob talking to me heightened my suspicions even further about you. But do you know what cinched it for me?"

"No."

He smiled and he looked like an animal baring its teeth. "Did you know that I've got cameras all over this place?"

"No I didn't."

"It was shortly after talking to Bob that I realized I was missing something from my desk, so I checked out my tapes to see who the thief was."

I didn't like the way this was going. How could I have been so stupid as to not notice the cameras? Were my rusty skills and my desire for the $10,000 going to cost me my life?

"You aren't the only surveillance specialist," he said

smugly. "I saw you break into this place, Mr. Whoever, so don't tell me that you did that because you were working for Bob Linehan Senior and he was worried about his precious little son—who can sure as hell take care of himself! That boy's a soldier! Tell me one thing before I kill you, and I am going to kill you: who are you really working for?"

Chapter 45

"I told you," I said, "I'm not working for anyone."

"I don't believe you! I have my suspicions about who your bosses are and if I'm right—" He began to laugh with a sinister look in his eyes, a laugh that was more frightening than any words the man could utter. "If I'm right then you're well-trained enough that you would never crack no matter how much torture I inflict upon you."

I was feeling close to cracking with the simple mention of the word torture. One always hopes to remain brave and strong in the face of such treatment but I was falling apart. "Please . . . please, don't hurt me. I have nothing to tell you. Nothing. I don't know anything. I'm sorry I broke in here but I was desperate for the money and—"

"Your first excuse was that you were just doing your job and now you were just doing it for the money. Do you really think that either of those excuses makes you any less guilty?"

I didn't know what to say and I told him so.

"I bet you know everything about me, don't you?" he asked.

"Not everything . . ."

He held up my digital camera. "I see that you were quite thorough when you came through here. You even took photos of me and my boys from our base in Kuwait. See?"

He turned the camera around and showed me the photo I took of the photo hanging on his office wall.

"I was over there. Two tours. You know much about that war?"

"Only what was on TV."

"Yeah, CNN loved Desert Storm, didn't they? The war made that network, or was it the network that made the war? There were TVs set up in goddamned shopping centers so that people wouldn't miss a minute of America's great new war! They made it seem like a swift and easy victory, unlike the mess they're in over there right now. They said we got in and out clean. You know how many Marines they say we lost over there?"

"No."

"Guess."

"Five hundred?"

"What? No way! Twenty-four! That's it! They also say that on top of that another forty-four died away from combat. Accidents, that sort of thing. Then they say that another ninety-two marines were injured. Pretty good numbers, right? Is that what you're thinking?"

I didn't know what to say since I was afraid that the wrong words might cause him to fly off the handle again. My insides and throat were still hurting from his earlier attacks and I wanted to do everything I could to prevent the pain from getting worse.

"The thing of it is, mystery man, is that those numbers are bullshit! It's all lies, man! Lies and bullshit piled on top of lies and bullshit! Half the soldiers that served over there came back screwed up, screwed up in ways that the best medical minds in America can't figure out, did you know that?"

"I-I did." Gord had mentioned it to me in the suburban when looking at Ray's file.

"And I know why. Do you want me to tell you?"

"Okay."

He leaned close and he spoke softly with minty breath. "Because the desert is hell and no one gets out of hell alive." He straightened up. "I saw from my tape that you looked in there—" He pointed to the wardrobe full of knives and swords. "So you saw the drawing, didn't you?"

"Yes."

"I saw the devil out there in the desert, do you believe that?"

"I-I don't know."

"Do you believe in God, Mr. Whoever?"

"I don't think so. I did once, but not for a long time now."

"I don't either, but I do believe in the devil and you would too if you'd seen him like the rest of us did that night. He's at work in our world, at work all over this world, and you can read all about him in the papers every day."

I thought of Bob Junior lying on the bank of the polluted stream, his waxen skin, his glassy eyes. "Yeah, I guess I know what you're talking about."

"We were called out when Saddam had his boys light the oil rigs on fire before they turned tail and left Kuwait. You ever seen a rig burning?"

"Only on TV."

"By the time we got there it was night but the fire burned so bright that it was like the area around the rigs was daytime, like someone had been messing with night and day. Liquid flames were getting pumped from the earth a few hundred gallons a second. Black hot wet flame. We weren't even that close but once we got back to base camp we saw that we were all covered in the black. Our clothes, our faces, every inch of us. It wasn't until I closed my eyes and tried to fall asleep that I realized I had seen something in the flames. I saw it again in my dreams that night. I never told anybody about it but the next day my best bud hands me a drawing and that's what I got hanging in there. He's a good artist for a soldier, right?"

"Y-yes."

"He says that the drawing was what he'd seen in his dreams the night before, and what he'd seen dancing in the flames at the top of the rig. It was the same goddamned thing I'd seen! How do you explain that?"

"I don't know."

He leaned close again and there was a fire in his eyes. "Because we did see the devil that night, mystery man. He's as real as you and me. The thing people don't know about him is that he's behind everything. Everything that this fucked up modern world calls progress is his work. The whole world is going crazy for oil, right? Our boys are over there killing and dying for it. Thick black foul burning liquid that flows from deep in the belly of the earth? Made from the bodies of dead and long-decayed plants and animals? Who else could invent something like that except for the devil?" He smiled and this time it seemed genuine. It was then that he pulled a short curved knife from behind him and held it beneath my chin. I lifted my chin as much as I could to get away from the blade but I could still feel its bite. "And I made a decision out there in the desert. If you can't beat him, join him."

"B-but what does this have to do with me?" I asked, trying to lift my chin upward away from the blade but smiling Ray kept the pressure on and I could feel fresh blood trickling down my neck.

"Do you work for the Company?"

"Wh-what company?"

"The Company. The CIA."

"Of course not!"

"You seem like the perfect agent. Always underfoot but at the same time invisible. A down-on-his-luck private investigator? A perfect cover."

"I-it's no cover. I'm just a regular guy trying to make a living."

"Did you kill Bob?"

"What? Of course not!"

"Did you kill him as a warning to me? A warning that you were closing in?"

"N-no, Ray. I never touched him."

He whispered into my ear. "Did you watch the DVD?"

"Yes."

"Did you understand what was happening?"

"B-Bob Junior was fighting a dog."

"You're such a simple-minded fool. Do you only see what's on the surface of things? Bob was doing battle with the dark forces of the devil, mystery man, the devil in the guise of a vicious dog. It takes guts, real courage to look the devil in the eye while armed only with a short blade, wouldn't you agree?"

"Yes."

He straightened up and said, "You're boring. I think I'll kill you now."

Chapter 46

There was a crash at the base of the stairs and Ray pivoted so that he was crouched behind me with the wicked blade against my throat. It sounded as if someone had kicked in the front door, breaking the glass.

Gordon Grossman appeared at the top of the stairs, a pistol in hand, a pistol he turned toward Ray and me.

"Drop the knife, Ray," he said.

"I'll kill him before I do that."

"You cut him with that blade and I'll shoot you."

"I'm not afraid to die."

"Good. I'm not afraid to kill you."

"Stay where you are!" Ray shouted and the knife bit into my neck and I could feel blood flowing from the new wound. "I'll cut him open if you don't put down your gun!"

Gord stood there a moment, and I wondered if he was contemplating taking the shot. Ray was hidden behind me and I doubted Gord could hit him, even at ten meters away.

"Okay," Gord said, lowering his pistol to the floor. "We can work this out, Ray. No need for anyone to die here tonight."

Ray laughed. "But where would the fun be in that, huh? Drop your belt too," he said and Gord did so.

"You're a fighter aren't you?" Gord asked. "A soldier?"

"I'm a marine."

"Then fight me, man-to-man. No one knows I'm here. I was just playing a hunch. If you beat me you can walk out of here."

"I don't want to fight you. I want you to watch me cut Mr. Nobody's throat!"

Again the knife bit, but not to kill. Ray was still just playing.

"You know you can't beat me, is that it?"

"You're bigger than me. Even with my skills and training, body mass still has its advantage. A middleweight isn't going to beat a heavyweight."

"Never thought a marine would back down from a fight."

"A marine isn't stupid either! He knows when the odds are stacked against him!"

"So what are we going to do here, Ray? How is this going to play out?"

Ray thought a moment then said, "Take off your bulletproof vest and put on your handcuffs."

"Why would I do that?"

"Do it or I'll kill him right now!"

I was doing my best to not cry out each time the knife cut me, but I was having a hard time not screaming in pain and fear. I didn't want to die.

"You okay, Lasker?"

"G-great," I managed to say.

"You look like shit."

"Really? I feel just super."

"I cuff myself and then what?"

"Then we fight. But if I beat you, I'm going to kill you and then kill your friend. You know that, don't you?"

"Yeah, you're making that pretty obvious, Ray."

"So what's it going to be? You put on the bracelets or I open his throat up right now."

"Okay, okay." He slowly reached out to his belt and removed his cuffs from the pouch on his belt. "We'll do it your way."

"No, Gord, just leave! Don't do this!"

"Shut up!" Ray yelled, grabbing my hair and yanking my head back.

Gord put the cuffs on his wrists and his face was filled with a hard cold look of hatred.

"I'm still going to beat you," Gord said, "Even with these cuffs."

"Tighter!" Ray barked.

Gord gave them each a couple more clicks.

"Now kick your gun and your belt away from you!"

Gord did so.

Only then did Ray stand up straight and step around me. I could see that there was a wide smile on his face. "This is going to be fun."

Gord was much taller than Ray, but both men were incredibly strong. They began to circle each other, with me just off to one side.

"Ray," I said, "Put down the knife!"

His grin widened. "Why the hell would I do that?"

"You already got him in cuffs!"

"I said I wanted to fight him, not fight him fair."

Chapter 47

Ray lunged and slashed downward. Gord jumped back out of the path of the blade and shot his foot out, aiming for Ray's head. Ray saw it coming, but it still caught him on the cheekbone, though not fully. He bounced backward smiling.

"I knew this would be fun," he said.

They continued to strike out at one another, but neither Gord's tree trunk legs nor Ray's blade hit cleanly. The problem was that Gord's glancing kicks did much less damage than Ray's blade and as the fight went on Gord was definitely losing. There were a dozen bloody wounds from the razor-sharp blade on his legs and arms.

As for me, the spectator, I felt helpless.

I knew that Gord was going to die and I was going to have to watch, and then I too would be killed. Why had Gord agreed to this ridiculous fight? Why didn't he just call in reinforcements and if Ray cut my throat so be it? It would be bad enough to lose my life but even worse to die knowing that an old friend had died trying to save me.

It quickly went from bad to worse for Gord.

He launched a side kick and Ray sidestepped it like a matador would a charging bull and he brought the knife down and slashed Gord's calf deeply, his first clean strike, and it drew a large amount of blood. Gord winced and Ray laughed.

"I'm going to chop down the tree!" he taunted.

Gord was having trouble putting weight on his injured leg that was seeping considerable quantities of blood, and it was making Ray bold. He was darting in and out, and more than once his short wicked knife nicked Gord's arms, legs and body, leaving the big man a seeping bloody mess.

It looked like Ray was toying with him. I thought that Ray could have executed a killing blow anytime he wanted, but being a sadist he was choosing to draw out Gord's death.

Blood was flowing from a dozen wounds on the big man and it was an awful thing to watch.

"Anytime you want to bow your head and die quick," Ray said, "I'll grant you that."

"Don't count on it, asshole."

"Just run!" I yelled, "Get the hell out of here!"

"That's not gonna happen," Gord said, his eyes never leaving his opponent.

"So noble!" Ray said, glancing between the two of us. "It almost makes me want—"

Ray was so pleased with himself, and so pleased to see Gord's blue uniform stained with blood and his face drained of color, that he'd become overconfident. Gord struck his opponent squarely in the solar plexus with the heel of his big black boot and it launched him several meters backward. Ray fell to the floor, eyes wide, gasping for breath, his hands to his chest. He rolled to his stomach in an effort to get to his feet.

Gord leapt forward and dropped onto Ray's back, like a fat kid doing a cannonball into the deep end of a swimming pool. The force of the blow must have broken several of Ray's ribs but he was not done fighting. Though he was facedown he swung his hand back and buried the knife into Gord's side, just above his right hip. Gord brought his hands down and brought the chain of the handcuffs around Ray throat and pulled upward with his considerable strength. Ray grasped hopelessly at the chain with his left hand and swung the knife backward, stabbing Gord in the side again and again. But halfway into the third strike Ray's hand fell to the floor, the knife skidding away. Gord's face was inhuman and he did not release the pressure of the chain for another minute, making sure that Ray was dead. When there was no doubt, he moved his hands and Ray's face hit the floor with a thump. Gord rolled off of him.

"Gord! Gord! Are you okay?"

"Yeah." He pulled himself along the floor to his belt, leaving a wet red trail behind him, and picked up his radio and struggled to speak. "Officer down. Second floor." He gave the address. "I've been stabbed. Need immediate assistance."

Within seconds I could hear a siren in the distance.

Gord then pulled himself toward me with a knife from his belt. His face was pale and it was obvious that his strength was fading. The floor was slick with his blood but still he was trying to get to me, trying to cut me free. The selflessness of his actions, and the relief at being alive had me crying like a child.

"Gord! Gord, just relax. Stay where you are." He still came forward. "I'm okay. They're coming to help you, buddy. You did it, you saved my life."

He was a meter away from me when he passed out.

Chapter 48

Drifting.
In and out of the fog.
"Mr. Lasker?"
Confusion. Sleep. Darkness.
A light in my eyes.
"How are you feeling, Mr. Lasker?"
No pain. I felt nothing. Complete numbness.
"Can you hear me?"
Yes, I could hear the man but was unable to respond; unable to ask what had happened to me, unable to ask if Grossman was dead or alive.
"Squeeze my hand if you can hear me."
I wasn't sure if I could manage that.
"Good, Mr. Lasker, very good."
Unable to open my eyes. Again to darkness.
From within the fog I could hear a television.
Strange: it seemed to be speaking about me.
"Details are still coming in about the death of American Desert Storm veteran Ray Iger who was killed in his Scarborough martial arts gym by a Toronto SIU officer."
Was I dreaming?
"According to police sources, he was injured in the process of rescuing Derek Lasker, a private investigator, who had been taken prisoner by Iger."
"That's you, ain't it?" came a voice from somewhere, but I was unable to respond. "Hey! Hey, it is! We got a famous man in our room!" A murmur of excited voices responded to that.
The television continued through the swirling murk. "The exact link between Iger and confessed murderer Robert Linehan Senior is still unclear. Linehan has confessed to

the murder of his son, Robert Junior, who was a student at Iger's martial arts gym. Private investigator Derek Lasker was working for Robert Linehan and may have been investigating Iger's links to underground fighting when the man captured him. We have been seeking a comment from Lasker, but he remains in hospital in stable condition."

Hospital? Stable?

I didn't feel stable. I felt like I could sleep for a thousand years and with that thought, I fell again into unconsciousness.

A phone was ringing.

I opened my eyes and saw I was lying in a hospital bed.

I brought my hands to my chest and it seemed that I was wrapped in enough bandages to make me feel embalmed, ancient Egypt style. I was in a room with three other beds, two of which had patients in them. To my left was a grinning old man with wild eyes.

"Well, well! Mister famous man is awake!" He began to laugh and his gap-toothed mouth made the moment feel quite surreal.

The ringing phone was on my bedside table so I picked it up.

"Hello?"

"Derek Lasker?"

"Yes?" My tongue felt dead in my mouth, making my voice thick, strange and unfamiliar.

"This is Marge Delahunt and I'm a producer at CNN. How are you feeling?"

I was still very confused and unsure what was real and what was fantasy. She continued speaking in her rapid-fire manner before I had the chance to respond.

"I've been leaving messages on your phone but I finally convinced the hospital operator to put me through to your room by telling her I was your beloved sister, so I'm going to get right to the point, okay?"

"Okay."

"We'd like to interview you and I want to know when you will feel healthy enough to do it. Tomorrow?"

"Interview?"

"A live interview, yes. If you agree I would ask you to refrain from speaking to any other news provider. Trust me, you will be adequately compensated for giving us an exclusive interview about Ray Iger and the time you spent as his hostage. We understand he had you tied to a chair?"

"Taped."

"Pardon?"

"He taped me to a chair."

"Well, that's just the sort of information that our viewers would love to hear. It's 8 p.m. now, so I'll call you first thing in the morning to see if you are up for a remote feed tomorrow, okay?"

I touched the bandages. "What happened to me?"

"That's exactly what I want you to tell our viewers."

I looked down at the phone in my hand and a dial tone was all I could hear. I put the receiver back.

I turned to the strange old man next to me. "Did I just talk to CNN?"

"Mr. Famous! They been talking about you on the news and everything!" The strange old man didn't help me at all.

What had happened to me?

The last thing I remember was Gordon crawling toward me then he passed out. I was feeling dizzy but what then? I had heard the sirens approaching but had no recollection of the police arriving. Before I could recall anything further, I was out again.

When I next opened my eyes the sun was shining through the window and I felt agony unlike anything I had experienced, and I had lived through some painful times. There was a ridiculous itching beneath the bandages on my torso and it made me feel like my skin was alive and trying to rip itself from the muscles beneath. I reached for the nurse's buzzer and pushed it. A moment later, a nurse in a garish Looney Tunes smock appeared.

"Well look who's awake!" she said with a smile.

I told her that I needed something for the pain, almost shouting at the poor woman. I don't like pain.

She took my tone in stride and kept on smiling and said, "Okay, give me just a minute."

I turned my head and saw that the bed to my left was empty, there was no strange old man. True to her word, the nurse was back in a moment and injected a syringe of something wonderful into my IV. The effect was remarkable and quick, like a cool shower in the dog days of August.

"What happened to me?"

"You got cut up pretty bad. Don't you remember?"

"No."

"The doctors said he did it to you before wrapping you in the tape. It was the only thing that saved your life."

I shuddered as his twisted smile flashed in my mind. Ray taped me up because he wanted me to die slow.

"Is Gordon Grossman okay?" I asked.

"He is. He's just down the hall and said he wanted me to inform him the moment you came around. Would you like to see him?"

"Yes."

"I'll be right back."

I thanked her and then the dizziness returned.

"I thought you said the lazy bastard was finally awake?"

The words pulled me from the darkness and I opened my eyes and saw Gord hulking above me with the nurse behind him. He was on his feet, but was leaning heavily on an aluminum cane.

"Gordo! I'm glad to see you. I was worried you were dead."

"Me? Dead? Haven't you figured out by now that I'm immortal?"

"Yeah, maybe you are."

"They say you were cut up pretty bad."

"I'll live."

"Good." Gord sat down at the foot of my bed, and he winced as he did so and the fact that he showed pain revealed just how hurt the tough man was. The whole bed shifted beneath his considerable weight.

"Did I hear the TV right? Bob Senior killed his son?"

"Yeah. Dorothy Linehan called Papineau and told her all about it. Said that the two were arguing and then he stabbed his son. He thought his wife was out of it on sleeping pills but she heard the whole thing. Apparently the old guy was having an affair with his neighbor and-"

"Ms. Johnson?" I asked. While listening to father and son argue on their driveway that day I had heard Bob Junior say that he had seen his father coming out of a motel with someone. It must have been Ms. Johnson.

"You know her?"

"I met her a couple of times."

"The son said he was going to tell Dorothy and Mr. Johnson about the affair. Linehan said this would destroy the big business deal he was lining up so..." Gordo shrugged.

"Jesus..." It seemed that the dog- and cat-killing son disapproved of his unfaithful father and was murdered because of it.

"He admitted to all of it once we sweated him for awhile. He drove the Civic to the apartment building hoping to put the suspicion elsewhere and then he dumped the body."

"And what about the cat head?"

"Linehan still says his son did it to hurt both him and Ms. Johnson and to let him know that he was serious. The stake the cat's head was on is the same as ones we found in the Linehan's tool shed, so that adds credence to the kid as cat-killer. Quite the psychotic kid."

"But whose tongue was in the cat's mouth?"

"As much as I hate to say it, we don't know. Not yet anyways. Someone involved with the underground fighting is my guess. We've turned the DVDs over to the RCMP and they're working with us on it. We've found the warehouse near Barrie where the fights happened and there's human blood all over the place. They even found two severed fingers in a corner. It wasn't just men fighting dogs. Men fought men and not all of them left the cage alive."

"Here in nice peaceful Canada!"

"Like I've been telling you, Lasky, if you knew just how foul people can be you'd want to crawl into a hole and die."

We were silent for a moment, chilled as we recalled the gruesome case.

"So what now?" I asked.

"We've already charged Bob Senior and the rest is up to the courts. And guess what, Lasky? The press is dying to hear from you. This case is big news. The fact that Ray was an American war veteran even has the US media up here covering the case. CNN is in town."

"Really?"

"Yeah, so anytime you're up for it we could call a nice little press conference downstairs, me and you together, and talk about this little adventure of ours. You could mention Lasker Investigations a few times and maybe get yourself some honest work. Make enough money to renew your license."

"What? I can't believe what I'm hearing. You're willing to share the spotlight?" I asked with a grin.

"Just this once," he said, returning my smile.

"That's gracious of you, Gordo, but I got a bigger offer, at least—" I scratched my head, uncertain as to whether the phone call from CNN was real "I think I do."

Acknowledgements

Thanks to early readers Heather, Evelyn and Glenn. Thanks to Mikael for lighting a fire under my ass. Thanks to my editors Gary Anderson and Julie Holaway for making this a better book.

About the Author

Born in Thunder Bay, Henry Brock lives in Toronto, where he works as a makeup artist for a number of popular daytime dramas.

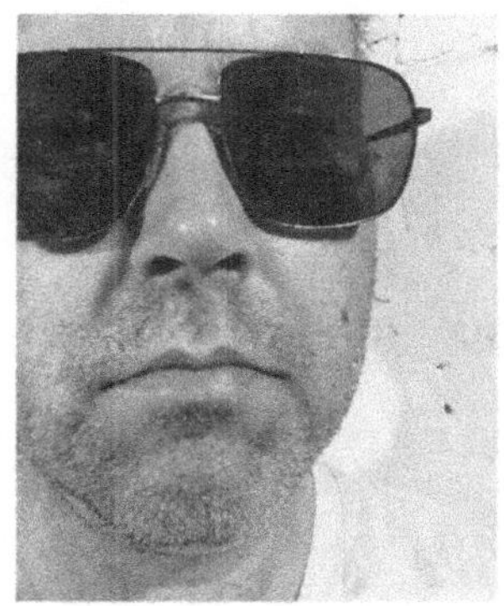

www.ingramcontent.com/pod-product-compliance
Lightning Source LLC
Chambersburg PA
CBHW061036120726
47910CB00006B/2271